BART HARDIN

Murder isn't Bart Hardin's official
business. Professionally he's a newspaper
editor. His side interests include
beautiful women, Irish whiskey, and
gambling on anything—a horse,
the turn of a card, the roll of dice.

But two hitches in the Marine Corps and a
lifetime spent on Broadway and its dark
environs have made Hardin a specialist
in violent death.

In DIE, LITTLE GOOSE, through
a tangle of conflicting and
murderous motivations, Bart
Hardin finds the amazing solution
to a clever and brutal crime.

DIE, LITTLE GOOSE
A BART HARDIN MURDER MYSTERY

Books by David Alexander

🐿 MURDER POINTS A FINGER

🐿 TERROR ON BROADWAY

🐿 PAINT THE TOWN BLACK

🐿 SHOOT A SITTING DUCK

🐿 THE MURDER OF WHISTLER'S BROTHER

🐿 Published by Bantam Books

A Bart Hardin Mystery

by

David Alexander

WILDSIDE PRESS

Die, Little Goose

Published by Wildside Press LLC
www.wildsidepress.com

TO A NICE LITTLE GOOSE
I KNOW NAMED ALICE

"Seven and crap," the stickman said. "Pay the line and pass the dice. Next shooter!"

The floating crap game operated by Moe Selig, Broadway's gambling czar, was being held that night in the cavernous recesses of a garage on West Fiftieth Street near Ninth Avenue. The place was shadow-haunted except for one small island lit harshly by a two-hundred-watt ceiling bulb. On the edge of the light pool, almost blending into the encroaching shadows, nine tense and sweating men squatted on their haunches, peering intently at the rough crap layout that had been chalked upon the cement floor. The atmosphere of the garage was as stifling and moist as that of a fetid cave, but the temperature was ten degrees lower than the 90 still being registered by street thermometers at ten-thirty in the evening. It was July and it was the thirteenth day of the worst heat wave in the history of New York City.

The stickman rolled six dice to Bart Hardin, a rangy man in his early thirties who served as managing editor of a sports and theatrical journal called the *Broadway Times* when he wasn't trying to beat an overlay at Belmont Park or fill an inside straight in stud or make Little Joe the hard way in the floating game.

Bart Hardin was not handsome, judged by the usual standards, but physically he was the kind of man who commands attention. There was a lean, hard look to him and a peculiar intensity, the intensity of the compulsive gambler. His short-cropped hair was so light it seemed silvery in contrast to the bronze pigmentation of his skin. His nose had been broken and it made a serpentine curve in the middle of his face that relieved the sharp, jutting angles of jaw and cheekbone. He had been born on Broadway, above a flea circus and fun arcade on Forty-second Street, where he still lived. He had never left Times Square except to serve two hitches in the Marines. He knew the Big Street in the way a card sharp knows a marked deck, and his familiarity with its denizens made him an odd mixture of toughness and tender-

1

ness, cynicism and naïveté. He could spot a phony at fifty
paces—and he was generally regarded as the softest touch on
Broadway.

Hardin went through the crapshooter's ritual of weighing
and pairing off the dice that had been thrust to him across
the cement. He chose two, rolled the four others back to the
stickman. He clutched the dice in a big fist and rattled them
close to his ear, trying to "listen to his luck" before he
made a bet. He had come into the game an hour and a half
earlier with what was left of the three-hundred-dollar weekly
salary he had received that afternoon. Taxes, social security
and other pestiferous deductions had already accounted for a
chunk of it and another fifty had gone to an old actor named
James Lennox. Lennox, who was in his middle seventies, had
been a friend of Hardin's father and he had been existing
on relief until Bart hired him as his "secretary" and paid
him out of pocket. The old actor could neither type nor
take shorthand, but Hardin claimed it was worth half a
yard a week just to look at an honest man on Broadway.

There was coarse money piled in front of Hardin now,
more than fifteen hundred dollars. On his last previous roll
he had let six hundred lay after a couple of "naturals,"
thrown Eighter from Decatur as his point and come up
double-four.

As Hardin hesitated, the stickman grew impatient. "Name
the bet, name the bet," he urged. "You can't get faded unless
you name your bet. If you don't lay it down, you can't pick
it up, and speculation is the life of trade."

Hardin was counting five hundred off his pile when there
was a sudden interruption. A stocky figure lumbered out of
the surrounding gloom, breathing heavily. It was Eddie
O'Grady, a Broadway character known as the Old Top Sarge,
who had been a hero of World War I and now served as
lookout for Selig's gambling enterprises.

Selig's face was pasty and moist in the glaring light as he
leaned forward and stared at the lookout. He said, "Don't
tell me it's the Law. I paid off plenty for the juice on this
floater and there ain't no stinking flatfoot slipping me the
Double-X."

Selig had been content to take the house percentage and
let the stickman, one of the Syndicate's expatriates from Vegas,
run the game, but now he was tense.

The Old Sarge said, "It ain't Law. It's some guy downstairs in the alley that wants to see Bart Hardin."

Hardin looked up at the Old Sarge, a sheaf of money in his hand. He said, "Who is it?"

The Old Sarge heaved heavy shoulders. "He didn't give no name. A young character and kind of skinny."

"He say what he wants?"

The Old Sarge shrugged again. "He's a friend of your secretary's, he says. He wants to tell you something, he says. He wants to tell you he just killed his wife."

Selig grinned unpleasantly, revealing yellow teeth. "Nice chums you got, editor," he said. "Only I wish you wouldn't make social appointments at the floater. The floater is supposed to be kind of private."

Hardin tossed the two dice back to the waiting stickman. He pocketed the money in his hand, scooped up the bills on the floor in front of him and stuffed those in his pocket, too. He said, "Pass the dice."

Selig said, "It's real lucky for you this jerk chilled his doll. Just at the right time, too. You're taking off with a bundle, Hardin."

Hardin made no answer. He buttoned the sweat-soaked collar of his shirt, slid his knit tie into place. He took a heat-rumpled raw-silk jacket off a peg on the wall where garage workers hung their overalls. He donned the jacket and followed the Old Sarge down a long ramp to the first floor of the garage. As he descended he could hear the dice rolling again and the muttered imprecations of the shooters. Murder was a minor distraction in the dedicated lives of gambling men, he thought.

The Old Sarge clicked back heavy bolts on a sliding steel door, cracked the door open a foot. He said, "I made him wait outside in the alley."

Hardin nodded and squeezed through the door. The areaway was lighted by a blue bulb over the door that cast an unearthly glow into the massed shadows. The humidity was wet wool on the city now and it held the city's million smells like a stagnant crucible. Even the stench of the garbage that burned eternally on the Jersey flatlands across the river was a part of it.

A slender, nervous young man stood just outside the door. He reeked of alcohol. He was many pounds underweight for his height and his dark eyes seemed bright and feverish even in the wan blue light. But in his own peculiarly intense way he was handsome. Hardin recognized him as a night-club dancer known as Adrian Temple. He and his crippled wife

Daphne lived in the room next to James Lennox at the relatively luxurious theatrical lodgings to which the old man
had moved when Hardin hired him.

"How did you know I was here?" Hardin asked the young
man.

Temple said, "Old Jim Lennox says you spend most of your
evenings at the Sligo Slasher's bar across from the Garden.
I went there. The little man who runs the place told me I'd
find you here."

"Why did you want to see me?" Bart asked.

"I've killed my wife, Hardin. I've murdered Daphne. I want
to confess."

"I'm neither a policeman nor a priest," Hardin said. "Why
confess to me?"

"I can't stand physical pain, Hardin. I'm a coward about
that. I've always been, ever since I was a kid. That's why I
couldn't go through with it. We had a suicide pact. I thought
I could get enough sleeping pills from the doctor, because
Daphne was paralyzed after the accident and she suffered
terribly at times. But he wouldn't give us enough. So I had
to kill her with a knife. When it came my turn, I couldn't go
through with it. I couldn't stand the thought of the pain,
even though I wanted to die. I went out and got drunk. I've
been drunk for hours now. I want to give myself up, but I
can't bear to have policemen beat me. I just want to die, to
pay for what I've done as quickly as I can. Old Jim told me
you know a police lieutenant named Romano. He says he's a
decent man. I want you to take me to him."

"Does Jim know you killed Daphne?"

"No one knows. I killed her about this time last night.
She's been there in her wheelchair dead for twenty-four
hours, Hardin, and nobody knows about it yet. I ran out of
the house and got drunk, and I'm still drunk. I just walked
and walked and walked when the bars were closed. I had a
bottle. I've been trying to work myself up to going to a
police station, but I was afraid they'd beat me. Then I thought
about you and how you knew the lieutenant. For God's sake,
take me to him, Hardin."

"Are you sure you killed your wife?" Hardin asked. "This
isn't just some drunken idea you've got?"

"Good God, man! Of course I'm sure!"

"But why?" asked Hardin. "Old Jim Lennox told me she
was doing as well as could be expected. He sees a lot of her.
He says she doesn't have much pain. And he told me you and

this new partner, Elsa, have just been booked for a spot in a night club starting next week."

"She wouldn't tell him how much she suffered, Hardin. She suffered terribly. She has, ever since that night I drove a car while I was drunk and smashed it up. I was thrown clear and was hardly hurt at all. But Daphne could never dance again. She couldn't even walk again. And it was my fault. We were a top act, Hardin. Adriane and Daphne, The Temple Dancers. This new girl and I, all we get is cheap hotel bookings and spots in strip joints."

"Romano's working the four to midnight," Hardin said. "He's at Homicide West on Twentieth. We can get a cab and drive downtown if you're sure that's what you want."

"I'm sure," Adrian declared.

As they walked down the alley, Hardin wondered why he was going out of his way to help a comparative stranger who was not only drunk but was probably a screwball. He hadn't wanted to leave the game. One of the gambler's ironclad axioms is "Stay in action when you're winning." He was doing this mainly because of old Jim Lennox, he supposed. Old Jim had seemed to like this boy and his crippled young wife, and to pity them. Hardin had always felt ironically paternal toward Lennox, who was some forty years his senior.

They walked toward Ninth Avenue. Two blocks back of them the brightest lights in all the world blazed on Broadway, but this neighborhood was cellar-dark. Men and women in underclothes and night dress leaned far out of the windows of brick and brownstone tenements, gasping for a breath of the stale air. In their despairing fight against the heat, they no longer lit their low-watt light bulbs, dreading to add even this small warmth to the choking pall inside their box-like flats. New York, Hardin thought, has the brightest lights and darkest byways of any city on earth.

At the corner of Ninth Avenue a red neon sign sputtered, flickering on and off, as if it, too, were melting in the heat.

The twisted tubes of the sign spelled out "Mike's Bar." Adrian paused at the corner. He looked at his wrist watch and said, "I've got to have a drink before I go through with this, Hardin. It's only ten to eleven. We've got time. Your friend will be on duty for another hour."

Hardin shrugged. "It's your party," he said.

Mike's place did not boast air conditioning. The door stood open and an electric fan on a tall standard blew swirling patterns of smoke and the stench of sweating bodies through the trapped air of the gloomy interior. Soiled men with dead faces stood at the bar, drinking silently. Adrian ordered a double shot of bar whisky and disregarded the water chaser the bartender placed beside it. Hardin refused a drink. While Adrian was drinking two doubles, Hardin said, "If the body has been there since last night, someone must have found it. I know your rooming house. It's a clean and decent place—one of the last of the old-fashioned Broadway theatrical residences—and Mrs. Mattingly wouldn't let a day go by without having your room cleaned. The maid must have been in there this morning. Jim drops by to chat with your wife all the time. He must have knocked on the door when he got home tonight after the paper was out. And your partner—Elsa Travers, is that her name?—lives in the room right next to you. She must have looked in, too, when you didn't show up today."

Adrian Temple said, "I can't understand why they haven't found the body, but I can't believe they have. I've read all the papers and there's nothing in any of them. They would have played it up. We were a famous dance team once. It was Daphne, though, who was the star. I was just her dancing partner. We had top billings everywhere. We were guest artists on all the big TV shows. We could name our own price then. We had an apartment on Park Avenue and a little hideaway in Connecticut and I drove an MG. I wrecked the MG when I was drunk and crippled Daphne for life. I was nothing without Daphne. She was the act. Since then, for two years now, I've tried a lot of partners and this last one, Elsa, is no better than any of the others. They book us to fill in between the strip women at cheap clubs. All our money's gone. The hospitals and doctors and operations took that."

He drank the last of his whisky and said, "They haven't found her yet. That's why I want to confess. I can't stand the thought of Daphne being there all alone, even though she's dead."

Hardin remained silent. Temple replaced his glass on the bar. His hand was shaking and his face had gone pale. He turned to Bart and said, "Hardin, it's not true what they say about electrocutions, is it? I mean, they don't give you the current slowly, torture you to death? I can't stand pain. I can't help it. It's a phobia. I've always been like that. I get sick all over at the thought of pain. They give you dope before they take you to the chair, don't they, Hardin?"

Hardin said, "I wouldn't know. I've never been electro-cuted."

Adrian glanced at the big clock on the wall. "It's eleven," he said. "We'd better go while I still have the courage, before the whisky wears off. I've got to go through with it now."

They left the bar and found a cab. Ninth Avenue is a one-way downtown street with staggered lights and they made good time. They reached Manhattan West in slightly under a quarter of an hour. The old precinct station was the clearing house for all the murders west of Fifth Avenue on Man-hattan Island. Appropriately enough, it was located in the edge of the area that used to be known as Hell's Kitchen.

The desk sergeant on duty was a pleasant, rather scholarly-looking man with horn-rimmed glasses and he might have resembled a high school Latin teacher if he had not worn a policeman's uniform. He knew Hardin. "If you want the lieutenant," he said, "you'll find him upstairs in his little sweatbox."

Hardin thanked the sergeant and led his companion up a flight of worn stairs.

Romano's office was an airless cubicle that contained a desk, two chairs and an old leather couch where the lieutenant, who seldom went off duty when a big kill was breaking, often slept. Romano sat in a creaking swivel chair behind the battered desk. He was in his shirt sleeves and his shirt was soaked. A small electric fan blew hot air at him. He was a dark, heavy-set man with a mane of black hair that was sprinkled with gray and shining with beads of perspiration. He perspired freely the year around and tonight he was drenched. His rough-hewn profile gleamed in the light of a green-shaded desk lamp. A tall young detective named Grierson reclined on the lumpy leather couch. His attire was less formal than Romano's. His crumpled shirt hung from the back of a chair and his undershirt gleamed white against his wide, sun-tanned shoulders. Grierson raised himself to a sitting position as Bart and Adrian entered the office.

Romano said, "Hello, editor. How are you enjoying our heat wave? And who's your friend?"

"This is Adrian Temple," Bart replied. "He wants to talk to you."

Romano looked hard at Adrian. He said, "I know you. I've seen you somewhere, not too long ago." He glanced toward Grierson and said, "You make him, Grierson?"

The young detective studied Adrian's face, shook his head.

"He's an entertainer," Hardin said. "A dancer. He was on television quite often up to a couple of years ago. Maybe that's why you recognize him."

Romano stared at Adrian. "No," he said. "I don't watch much of anything but ball games on TV. Ball games and the Disney show. I'm a sucker for Disney." He spoke directly to Adrian. "A dancer. I make you now," he said. "You were in here about six months ago, around the first of the year. You had a big load on. You wanted to tell me you'd killed your wife. We checked up. Your wife was an invalid in a wheelchair, but she wasn't dead. She was sitting in her wheelchair reading a book when the cops got there. We sent you to the city hospital for observation. They kept you there four or five days and let you loose. They said you were just drunk."

Romano turned to Grierson, said, "You make him now?"

Grierson nodded. "I remember. You think—"

Romano raised his hand to silence Grierson. He said to Adrian, "You want to confess another murder?"

Adrian's eyes were glazed. He seemed hardly conscious of what the lieutenant had said. He spoke in a monotone. "I want to confess the murder of my wife," he said.

Grierson said, "I'm damned."

"When did you kill your wife?" Romano asked quickly.

"Last night. About this time. A little earlier, I think. Somewhere between ten and eleven o'clock. We had a suicide pact, but I couldn't go through with my part of it after I'd killed her. I'm afraid of pain and the only weapon I had was a knife."

"You killed her with a knife?"

"I stabbed her through the heart."

"Where is the knife?"

"I—I don't know. I must have thrown it away. I got drunk and wandered around the streets all last night and today and then I found Hardin and asked him to bring me here to you so I could confess. For God's sake promise me you won't let them give me a third degree. I'm willing to tell you everything. I'm willing to die for what I did. But don't hurt me!"

Romano spoke almost pleasantly. "Relax," he said. "We don't use the third degree any more, except on known hoods and cop-killers, maybe. Tell me, where did you kill your wife?"

"In our room. We live on West Fifty-third Street. Mrs. Cora Mattingly is the landlady."

"Same as last time," Romano commented. He said to Grierson, "That checks?"

"It checks," Grierson answered.

"Get Farber from the squad room," Romano said.

Grierson did not bother to don his shirt. He walked out to the squad room and returned presently with the detective named Farber. Farber had a weatherbeaten face and large, sad eyes. He was mopping perspiration from his face with a blue bandanna handkerchief.

Romano said, "Farber, take this man outside and keep him there until I call you. He's not to be questioned or touched. Just watch him, that's all. He may be an important witness."

Farber nodded. He said to Adrian, "This way," and led him out of the office.

Romano regarded Bart quizzically. "How long has this man been with you?" he asked.

Bart looked at the stainless-steel watch on his wrist. "The better part of an hour. About forty-five minutes, anyway. He picked me up a little after ten-thirty."

Romano tapped his fingers on his desk. He and Grierson exchanged glances. The lieutenant said to Bart, "Two minutes before you walked into this office a routine precinct squeal came in. There was suspicion of murder at a rooming house on West Fifty-third Street. The house was operated by a woman named Cora Mattingly. She put in the call. The precinct men were on their way there. The way these things work, the precinct gets the squeal and buzzes us immediately. It's kind of an alert to Homicide, but we don't go out on it. We wait until the precinct men check. Half the time it's only a jumper or an accidental death or somebody's idea of a joke. If it looks like murder we get another call. When that comes through, Homicide sends a man and so does the D.A.'s office. Verification should be coming through in a minute or two now."

The verification came almost immediately. The phone on Romano's desk began to ring as he finished speaking.

Romano said to Grierson, "Take it."

Grierson picked up the phone. He answered, nodded affirmatively at Romano. He listened intently, scribbled on a pad, muttered meaningless monosyllables. Presently he said, "Okay, will do." He hung up the phone.

"A woman named Daphne Temple was murdered in Mrs. Cora Mattingly's rooming house on West Fifty-third Street," Grierson said in a flat voice.

"Then Adrian was telling the truth this time," Bart said. "I thought he was just drunk."

"No," said Grierson, "he wasn't telling the truth. The woman wasn't stabbed. She was shot through the heart. She wasn't killed last night. She was killed about twenty-five minutes ago, at five minutes to eleven. The landlady and a woman named Elsa Travers can establish the time exactly. They'd been to the show at the Music Hall. There's a grandfather clock in the hall of the house and when they came in they looked at it. A minute later they heard a shot and rushed upstairs. They found Daphne Temple dead with a hole in her heart and blood all over her."

Romano said, "Put your shirt on, Grierson. We'll go up there. I'll have Farber keep this Adrian Temple on ice. I want to question him some more before we let the bug doctors look him over again."

Grierson said, "There's something else."

"What?" Romano asked.

Grierson turned to Hardin. "You aren't going to like this, I'm afraid," he said. "What's the name of that old actor you keep on the payroll? The one you call your secretary? I met him a while back when the lieutenant and I dropped around to see you at the *Broadway Times*."

Hardin's eyes grew hard. "Lennox," he said. "James Lennox. He's a fine old man."

Grierson said, "James Lennox has the room next to the one where they found the body. He was standing on the fire escape outside Daphne Temple's room when Mrs. Mattingly and this Elsa Travers got there. The cops found a gun on the fire escape, about where he was standing. It was still warm, and the smell of the barrel confirmed the fact it had been fired at about the time the two women heard the shot. Ballistics will check it, but there's not much doubt it was the gun that killed Daphne Temple. The precinct boys are holding Lennox on suspicion of murder."

two

"How stupid can cops get?" Hardin asked bitterly.

Romano's dark Italian eyes regarded the editor sadly. He knew Hardin well and he knew that he was dangerously angry now. "Pretty stupid, I guess," he answered mildly, hoping a soft answer would turn away wrath.

Hardin was not to be placated. The bronze skin beneath his close-cropped blond hair was darkly flushed. "Charging old Jim Lennox with murder is as silly as accusing Grandma Moses of juvenile delinquency," he said. "I've known him ever since I was born. He's the last of a disappearing breed on Broadway—a gentleman. He was in the theatre at the turn of the century and he stayed in it until a guy named Stanislavsky came along and started something called the naturalistic school of acting which meant actors were supposed to stumble around the stage with their heads averted from the audience and mumble their lines. Jim thought the playwright had a right to have the lines he'd written heard and he thought the customers in the back row of the balcony had a right to hear them. His type of acting wasn't fashionable any more. But his knowledge of Broadway and the theatre has been worth a lot to me on the paper. Old Jim has lived for three-quarters of a century and he's been about as decent a human being as God ever made. He's so kindly and gentle he's practically out of this world. Nobody ever had a word to say against him until some pea-brained precinct cop comes along and calls him a murderer."

"Sometimes these sweet-faced old pappy guys do funny things," Grierson put in. "Especially when they get as old as this Lennox and there's a young chick around."

"Keep your goddamn mouth out of this, copper," Hardin said furiously. "I'm talking to the lieutenant."

Romano held up a restraining hand. "Don't flip your wig, editor," he said. "Not until the votes are counted, anyway. I know old Lennox. I've known him ever since I've had the Broadway beat, and that's been an awful lot of years. I like him. But don't blame the precinct men too much. Two people

11

hear a shot. They find a woman dead with blood all over her. They see a man standing outside her window and there's a gun at his feet that's just been fired. You can't just overlook a thing like that." He turned to Grierson, who was glaring at Bart. "Put your shirt on," he said. "We're gonna have to go uptown and the new commissioner don't like for Homicide dicks to go out on squeals in their underwear."

Hardin said, "I'm going up there with you. I've got a police pass that the department issues to newspapermen. It should entitle me to that. If you let these chowderheads take Jim Lennox in I'm going to get him a lawyer. I just won enough in the floater to afford a retainer for Marty Land."

"That pass don't entitle you to much of anything except to go through police and fire lines if the policemen and firemen want to let you through," Romano answered. "But I've got no objection to you going along. After all, the old guy works for you. Only I want to talk to this Adrian Temple some more first. Tell Farber to send him in."

Grierson had donned his shirt. He walked from the room, stuffing shirttails into trousers. He returned with Adrian Temple. Farber stood behind them in the doorway.

Romano regarded Adrian for a moment before he spoke. "I've got bad news for you, Temple," he said. "Your wife is dead."

Adrian dropped his head. For a moment his body shook with silent sobbing. Then he said, "It's true, then. I knew it was true this time. But I still hoped it would be like the last time, that I only dreamed it."

"You still think you killed her?" Romano asked. "Tell me again. When did you kill her? How?"

"I stabbed her to death about twenty-four hours ago," Adrian answered. "I've told you that. I confess. For God's sake do whatever you've got to do. Lock me up and get it over with. I'll sign anything you want. Only don't let them beat me."

Romano said, "Nobody's going to beat you. Where were you at about five minutes to eleven tonight?"

"Tonight?" Adrian looked at Romano in perplexity. Then he looked at his watch. "Why, I guess I must have been with Hardin here."

Hardin nodded. "That's right," he said. "We were in a bar called Mike's at the corner of Ninth and Fiftieth."

Romano said, "Take him out, Farber, and keep him on ice. If you go off duty, leave him with somebody. I may want to

talk to him later on. Then we're going to send him to the
psycho ward and see if the bug doctors can figure out why
he's always coming down here and confessing to murders."

Adrian stared at the lieutenant. "But you said she's dead!"
he protested. "I killed her!"

"Yeah," Romano answered. "Your wife is dead. And I'm
kind of sorry you've got an alibi from a solid citizen like
Hardin here. It's going to make a lot of work for me in this
hot weather."

Farber led the protesting Adrian out again. Romano,
Grierson and Hardin went to the street and got into a police
car. Grierson drove them to the rooming house on Fifty-
third Street near Sixth Avenue. It was one of the last brown-
stones in the neighborhood. The darkened basement was
occupied by a theatrical costumer who displayed suits of
armor and a collection of antique feathered hats in his
window. The house was in relatively good condition, although
the sandstone had weathered and the gargoyles that decorated
its posts and lintels were chipping away, giving the grotesque
faces a mutilated look.

The three men climbed out of the police car and mounted
a high stoop, where a uniformed policeman stood guard. The
window in the oak door was covered by a lace curtain. The
policeman recognized Romano. He saluted and opened the
door.

The dusky hallway was lighted by a small bulb that glinted
through a stained-glass shade. It was darkly carpeted and
decorated with potted ferns and yellowing photographs of
theatrical personalities. A grandfather clock and carved
wooden chairs were in the hallway. Aside from air-conditioned
bars and theatres, it was the coolest place Hardin had found
during the thirteen days of the heat wave. The house had
been constructed in the days when builders made walls thick
as protection from the cold and pitched the ceilings high
to minimize the summer heat.

A folding door opened into the first-floor parlor, where
several persons were gathered. Cora Mattingly sat in a high-
backed chair, answering the questions of a white-haired
detective who stood beside her with a notebook in his hand.
She was a plump woman in her sixties with an apple-round
and apple-rosy face and an abundance of lavender-washed
white hair that had been set into mathematically precise
ridges and curlicues by her hairdresser. She dabbed at moist
eyes with a wispy handkerchief and the motion of her tiny,

pudgy hand was graceful. Hardin remembered that she had once been an actress in a Shakespearean repertory company.

A tall, slender girl stood behind Mrs. Mattingly, clasping the landlady's shoulder with a bony hand. Her blood-red nails gleamed like jewels against the soft gray of Cora Mattingly's dress. Hardin recognized the girl as Elsa Travers, Adrian Temple's latest dancing partner. She had a gaunt, peculiar beauty. She affected an Italian bob and spikes of her black hair spilled down on a high white forehead. Dead-white make-up emphasized the triangulated bone structure of her face, whose pallor was relieved only by the crimsoned mouth that was over-large and by the dark, unswept penciling of her brows and eyes. She wore a dark jersey dress that fit her as tightly as a dancer's leotards and her sharp breasts thrust nakedly against the material. Her only jewelry was a heavy silver chain that circled her waist. The buckle was set with an enormous imitation topaz.

Jim Lennox sprawled upon a Victorian love seat near the baroque marble mantelpiece. He was a tiny man, barely five and a half feet tall, and he seemed as fragile and delicate as a Sèvres figurine. His thick white hair hung down his neck and curled over the opened collar of his shirt in an antiquated theatrical fashion that had only lately been revived by young hoodlums and television actors and was called a ducktail haircut. Even in his most poverty-stricken days the old man had always been neat and chipper. Now he was rumpled and frightened and he seemed utterly defeated. His usually keen old eyes were dimmed by bewilderment and shock.

A fat detective who was sweating profusely stood beside the little man, apparently guarding him. The contrast between the prisoner and his keeper was almost ludicrous. The tableau made Hardin think of a lumbering St. Bernard mothering an undersized Chihuahua.

Recognition swam into Lennox's eyes as Bart entered. "Bart!" he cried, rising from the small sofa. "For God's sake, Bart! These policemen think I'm a murderer!"

Bart tried to think of something reassuring to say. Before he could speak, the white-haired detective was addressing Romano. "Hello, Lieutenant," he said. "You're just in time. We're about to take the statement of the ladies who discovered the body and heard the shot. This is the landlady, Mrs. Mattingly, and Miss Travers." He turned to the woman on the chair and said, "Now just try to compose yourself, ma'am,

and let's go over it again. This is an officer from Homicide
and he'll want to hear what you have to say."

Mrs. Mattingly choked back a sob, dabbed at her eyes.

"I've told it so many times already," she said.

"Tell us about the house and the roomers first," the precinct
detective prompted.

"There are five rooms in the house that I rent out,"
Mrs. Mattingly said, pressing her fingers to her temple as if
she were trying to squeeze the story from her mind in proper
sequence. "I occupy an apartment on this floor. There are
three rooms and a bath and a linen closet on the second. The
first, the smallest room, is occupied by Mr. Lennox here.
The largest room was occupied by Mr. Adrian Temple and
his wife Daphne, who was—was murdered. She was an invalid. The third room is occupied by Mr. Temple's dancing
partner, Miss Travers, who is here with me. My daughter
has a small apartment on the top floor but it is unoccupied
now because she's playing stock in Louisville. The other two
rooms on the top floor are rented to Mr. Montgomery and
Mr. Sandrean. Mr. Montgomery is a ventriloquist who con-
ducts the 'Woodenhead Willie' program for children over
television. Mr. Sandrean is a Mexican gentleman who is a
magician. He is known professionally as El Diablo. Neither
gentleman was home this evening. In fact, no one was home
except poor Daphne and James Lennox. I shouldn't have
gone to the theatre."

Mrs. Mattingly was weeping and dabbing at her eyes with
her wispy handkerchief again. "Now, now," the detective
said soothingly. "You shouldn't blame yourself, ma'am."

"We had these tickets to the Music Hall," she continued.
"Mr. Sandrean—El Diablo, that is—has a spot in the current
stage show and he gave us tickets for everyone in the house,
except poor Daphne, of course. Even Adrian, Mr. Temple,
was going with us. He thought he could find some friend to
sit with Daphne. But yesterday Mr. Temple had one of his
little disappearances, as I call them. Adrian has a weakness,
poor, unfortunate man. He drinks at times. When he does,
he simply wanders off for a day or two. We've come to expect it every few months. He is still missing, in fact. Of
course, we didn't like leaving Daphne alone. My maid comes
in days and she leaves around six as a rule. Elsa offered to
stay with Daphne, but Daphne wouldn't hear of it. She
wouldn't hear of any of us missing the show, in fact. She said

her husband would probably return anyway, because she knew his habits when he's on one of his little sprees.

"Then Mr. Lennox came back from his office, all done in by this terrible heat. He has a slight heart condition and he looked pale and wretched. He said he had a terrible headache and was going to lie down. That solved the problem. His room is right next to the one the Temples occupy. James often sits with Daphne when Adrian and Elsa have an engagement at a club. If Daphne needed anything, she could call or tap on the wall. She's very self-reliant, really, and gets around quite well in her wheelchair."

The plump little woman gasped and shivered. The bony hand with the blood-red nails patted her shoulder comfortingly.

When Mrs. Mattingly recovered, she continued, "Mr. Montgomery, the ventriloquist, accompanied Miss Travers and me to the theatre. I'm afraid two tickets went to waste. The ones that Mr. Sandrean had given Adrian and Mr. Lennox. After the show Mr. Montgomery invited us to a bar for refreshment, but Elsa has been feeling the heat and she wished to get home and shower and retire early. Mr. Montgomery left us to go for a drink. I suppose we must have left the Music Hall about a quarter to eleven. It's only three blocks from here, you know. Anyway, we were home at seven minutes to eleven exactly. I know, because I have a habit of glancing at the big grandfather clock in the hall. And it's always right. It was just a couple of minutes later that it happened."

She paused again, overcome by emotion. Then she said, "Elsa went directly upstairs to go to her room. I came into the parlor and turned on the lights. A few seconds after Elsa reached the top of the stairs, I heard this shot. I ran out into the hall. Elsa was screaming, calling me. I rushed upstairs. We hesitated a moment, trying to guess where the the shot had come from, calling Daphne. We went into Daphne's room. She was there in her wheelchair, dead, covered with blood." Mrs. Mattingly buried her face in her hands and sobbed.

"And Mr. Lennox was standing on the fire escape, staring at poor Daphne," Elsa Travers said, her chalk-white face grim.

Bart turned to the stricken old man on the love seat. He said, "Can't you explain this, Jim?"

"I have explained it, Bart. But they won't believe me,"

Lennox answered. "You thought I looked peaked and you sent me home early from the paper. I stopped at the Automat and had a salad and some tea. It was all I felt like eating. My blood pressure has been acting up in this heat. I came home and the others were going to the Music Hall to see El Diablo. I simply wasn't up to it. I said I would stay home with Daphne. After they left for the theatre I looked in on Daphne. She was well, but she was drowsy. She didn't want me to help her onto the bed. She felt sure Adrian would return this evening and she wanted to be sitting up when he arrived. She said he was always remorseful when he came home after he had been drinking and she wanted to be awake to comfort him.

"I hardly slept at all last night. Tonight I took some medicine the doctor gave me for my blood pressure condition. There's a mild sedative in it, I think. I lay down on my bed without undressing. I didn't lock my door. No one here ever does. The keys are almost always on the outside of the doors, in fact, until we retire for the night. I left mine on the outside. I got up once and looked in on Daphne. She was dozing in her chair. I went back in my room about nine and lay down on the bed again. I was stupefied by the heat or the sedative, and I fell into a deep sleep. The shot awakened me. I thought of Daphne at once. Then I heard someone screaming and calling Mrs. Mattingly's name. I tried to get out my door, but it was locked from outside, so I went out on the fire escape to get into Daphne's room through the window. I saw her there in the chair, with blood on her. I could smell the smoke from the shot. I guess I was frozen stiff with horror. The door to Daphne's room opened and Cora and Elsa came in. Cora rushed downstairs to call the police and then Elsa left, but I just stood there, stupefied, until the police came. This policeman says he found a gun on the fire escape where I was standing. I didn't see the gun. You know I wouldn't own a gun."

The fat, sweaty policeman said, "The gun was up against the rail of the fire escape, like somebody had tried to kick it off but hadn't pushed it far enough."

The white-haired policeman said, "Tell them about the door, Mrs. Mattingly."

The plump landlady bit her lips. Finally she said in a faint voice, "When James told me the door was locked, I tried it. The key was on the outside but it hadn't been turned. It wasn't locked."

Bart said, "In this humid weather doors are warping and sticking all over the city. Jim tried the door and it stuck and he thought it was locked, so he rushed out on the fire escape, that was all."

"Did the door stick when you tried to open it, Mrs. Mattingly?" the white-haired detective asked.

Mrs. Mattingly looked despairingly at Lennox. "Oh, James," she said, "I hate to do this to you. I know you're no murderer. I know you loved Daphne as we all did." She looked at Bart. "James Lennox is one of my oldest friends, Mr. Hardin. You know that. We trouped together in Mantell's Repertory more than thirty years ago. But I have to tell the truth. The door wasn't stuck. It opened quite easily."

The precinct officer addressed Romano. "The body's upstairs, Lieutenant," he said. "Along with an assistant M.E., and an assistant D.A. and I.D. men and some more plain cops. Maybe you want to take a look."

Romano nodded. Grierson and Hardin followed him up the stairs. At the top of the stairs, the door to Lennox's room stood open. Policemen were ransacking it. It was a fair-sized room and it was comfortably furnished. The window opened on a fire escape and an airshaft and faced the blank wall of the next buliding, but Bart knew that a peculiar downdraft in the areaway made it airy except in this still, hot weather. The old man who had endured grim poverty for many years had found a haven here with Bart's help. The walls were covered with theatre programs, framed pictures of himself and other actors in scenes from forgotten plays.

The next room, much larger, was the one occupied by Adrian and Daphne Temple. It had windows on both the front and side of the house. In front was a bath and Elsa Travers' room and a large linen closet.

Even in the pallor of death, Daphne Temple seemed petite and childish. She lolled in her chair now, her back to the wall behind the bed, her profile to the window on the fire escape. She had been shot at close range through the heart. There was a great dark stain drying on the blue silk robe which she wore over a lace nightgown. Her eyes were closed as if she had been sleeping when a murderer's bullet blasted her life away.

An identification man held up the gun on a peg board for Romano's inspection. "Army forty-five," he said, "with the serial number filed off. It was warm when the precinct man found it and the barrel smelled of cordite. Two shots fired. No sign of the other one. It might have been fired at some other time, of course. The slug went right through her and imbedded itself in the back of the chair." He palmed a misshapen pellet, showed it to the lieutenant. "We pried it out. This is it. It's a forty-five, that's for certain. Ballistics can tell us more."

The assistant D.A. was a youngish, tired-looking man named Senber. He had deep, liverish circles beneath his eyes. "Well, you Homicide guys have got an easy one this time," he said. "It's too hot to work hard, anyway. They found the old man on the fire escape a second after he chilled her, and he told a lot of lies about locked doors to explain how he got there."

"You think you've got enough to ask for an indictment?" Romano asked.

"Enough?" the D.A. said. "How much you want? This is what you cops call catching a criminal with the meat in his mouth. Don't try to make it complicated. It's too damned hot for complications."

Romano turned to the medical examiner. He was a spindly, middle-aged man who did not seem to be affected by the heat. His cord suit was crisply creased and his white collar wasn't wilted. Romano said, "Anything to tell me, Dr. Grew?"

Grew shrugged. "It's pretty cut and dried," he answered. "I never say too much about the probable time of death without an autopsy. That would be particularly hard because of the blood coagulation and so forth of a woman who is paralyzed. But it's a cinch she wasn't killed very long ago and the time of ten fifty-five that is set by the two women who heard the shot would be just about right, I'd think. Oh, there's one queer thing."

"What?" Romano asked.

The M.E. leaned forward and plucked a small object off the blue robe. "Feathers," he said. "White feathers like this one. We found a few of 'em. Some were stuck to the wound. Some others were on the robe or scattered around her feet and a few were on the fire escape where the old man was standing."

Romano took the feather. "Feathers," he said. He handed it to Grierson. "You make anything out of this feather, Grierson?" he asked.

Grierson looked at the feather briefly.

"I can tell you one thing," he answered. "I can tell you what kind of feather it is. My brother-in-law runs a poultry farm on Long Island, and I go out there a lot.

"This is a goose feather."

three

Two young men in white coats arrived, and at a nod from the medical examiner they began to lift the small body from the wheelchair onto a canvas stretcher. Hardin turned abruptly and walked out into the hall. Romano followed him.

Romano said, "Don't take it too hard, honey boy. The jury isn't in yet. Like I told you, I've known the old man a long time and I'll give him every break I can."

Bart said, "Are you really going to charge this old man with murder, copper?"

Romano shook his head despairingly. "Don't make it so personal," he said. "I don't charge anybody with anything. I take 'em in, that's all. You heard what the D.A. said. He wants me to take Lennox in. There won't be any charge yet, not right away. At this stage we just say we're holding them for questioning."

"No matter what you call it, you're arresting him on suspicion of murder," Bart answered. "That will kill him. You won't need the services of the executioner up at Sing Sing. It's not just his heart and his blood pressure and this heat will do it. All that he has left is the memory of a long and blameless life and you're taking that away from him. You're not only labeling him a murderer, you're implying he's a detestable old man who killed a helpless, crippled girl for a dirty reason. There couldn't be any other kind of reason for a man his age to kill a girl the age of Daphne."

Romano regarded Hardin sadly. "You're making me out a villain because I happen to have the rank and it's my responsibility to take him in," he said. "I'm not a villain. I'm just a cop and cops have to do nasty things sometimes. I can't expect you to see it the way a cop has to look at it, but just the same I'm going to lay it on the line for you. Two women hear a shot fired. One of them is standing right outside the door of the room where the gun went off. Nobody comes out the door. There's one other way out of the room —through the window and down a fire escape. They open the door and they find a dead body and they find a man standing on the fire escape just outside the window. The

21

man is James Lennox. A few minutes later a cop finds a gun
that probably fired the shot on the fire escape right where
James Lennox has been standing. Lennox claims he's standing on the fire escape because it was the only way he could
get out of his room when he heard the shot. He says his
door was locked from the outside. But the landlady who's
been a friend of his for thirty years and wants to help him
if she can has to admit that she tried the door, that it wasn't
locked, that it opened easily. You think the D.A.'s office is
going to let a Homicide lieutenant talk them out of taking
Lennox in just because he's a nice old man and has got a
blood pressure condition?"

"But damn it all, another man confessed he murdered
Daphne Temple!"

"Yeah," said Romano. "And you're the one who gave the
other man a perfect alibi. He was standing alongside you
in a Ninth Avenue bar when the murder was committed, you
said. You think he killed her by remote control or something?"

"I think it's damned suspicious that Adrian Temple confessed he killed his wife and we found her murdered."

"He confessed he killed his wife last winter and she lived
for about six months after that," Romano answered. "Adrian
Temple is a screwball with what they call an obsession. The
only reason the medics at City didn't bug him last time was
that everybody is flipping his toupee these days and there's
a shortage of beds in the loony bins. They wrote him off as
a harmless drunk and let him go after they'd hit his knee
with a little hammer a time or two."

Hardin said, "I'm going downstairs and talk to Jim Lennox. Then I'm going out to get him a lawyer. I'm going
to get him Marty Land."

"You're getting him a good one," Romano replied. "Marty
Land's just about the smartest cookie they ever baked in these
parts."

As Hardin descended the stairs the policeman on guard at
the front door walked into the hallway with a well-dressed,
jaunty young man. He called to the precinct detective, "This
guy claims he lives here."

Mrs. Mattingly walked into the hall to identify the new-
comer. Hardin, who had visited often in the house, recognized
the young man as Charlie Montgomery, the ventriloquist who
conducted a kids' show on television.

Montgomery said, "What's this all about? Why all the

gendarmes? Nobody kidnapped my dummy, Woodenhead Willie, did they?"

Mrs. Mattingly had regained some control of herself. Instinctively she had reverted to her role of actress as a defense mechanism in the emergency. When she spoke to Montgomery her voice was hollow-toned, like the portentous voice of Lady Macbeth on the night of Duncan's murder. "Charles," she said, "there's terrible news. Daphne was murdered while we were at the theatre."

The young man stared at her with disbelief for a moment. Then he paled and said, "Oh, my God, no!" and collapsed into a black walnut armchair.

Hardin walked into the Victorian parlor.

Lennox still sat on the little sofa, his face as white as his long hair, his eyes staring with bewilderment. The fat, sweaty detective hovered over him. The old man looked up at Hardin. "Bart," he said, "they're going to arrest me, aren't they? They're going to put me in jail. I've gone through a lot of human experiences in my time, but this is a thing I simply can't believe. Did you talk to our good friend Romano, Bart? Does he actually believe I would murder Daphne? I loved her, Bart. She was sweet and gentle and brave and I loved her very much."

Hardin's voice was harsh and edgy, as it always was when he was deeply moved. He said, "It's just routine. They have to take you in for questioning. I'm leaving now to get Marty Land to act as your attorney. Just don't worry. It'll be straightened out in no time."

"But Land is a very expensive lawyer, Bart. I can't afford his fees. I think the courts will appoint an attorney to represent me without charge."

"Land is representing you," Bart said curtly. "I won enough in the floater tonight to afford his retainer."

"You're a good man, Bart," Lennox said. "But I can't let you do this. I can't let you spend a lot of money for my defense. It isn't worth it. My old life can't be of much value now. There's too little left of it."

Hardin turned his back to keep Lennox from seeing his face. He said, "Nuts. Just remember to keep your chin up, that's all I ask of you. You told me once that Rostand's *Cyrano* was your favorite play. Act the part of Cyrano and remember your unblemished plume."

Bart walked hurriedly from the big room. In the hallway

he encountered Sandrean, the Mexican magician who was known professionally as El Diablo. The guard had just ushered him through the door. Sandrean was a dumpy, swarthy little man in his forties. He had none of the leanness and glib suavity that is usually associated with prestidigitators. To compensate for his unimpressive appearance and to justify his stage name, he had grown a Dali antenna of a mustache with waxed points and had supplemented it with arrowhead chin whiskers. Still he resembled a jolly, well-fed friar far more than he resembled Mephistopheles.

Cora Mattingly was still playing the role of tragic heroine. Her tones were sepulchral as she related the story of the murder to her roomer. Sandrean's reaction to the news was startling.

A stricken look came into his face and he spoke softly, as if he were addressing some person in the shadows of the hallway. "I knew it would happen," he said. "Something terrible was certain to occur. It is all my fault."

"What do you mean?" the white-haired detective asked quickly.

"The Feathered Serpent," the magician said. "It is because of the Feathered Serpent that she died."

The precinct man said, "What's this about feathers?"

"The Feathered Serpent Illusion," El Diablo replied, as if he were still addressing some unseen presence. "I should have known there would be a horrible vengeance for my sacrilege. The old gods are mighty ones. They are not to be mocked. But I went ahead. The Music Hall was a great opportunity for me and I wanted to be impressive, you see, so I invented the new illusion, the Illusion of the Feathered Serpent. I did not wish to perform only the old tricks. I worked a long while to perfect the new illusion. Instead of merely causing rosebushes to grow in thin air, I produced the Feathered Serpent from a receptacle no larger than a matchbox. It was eight feet in length and thick as a fire hose and it was covered with rainbow feathers like a peacock. Even the great Blackstone never produced so ambitious a mechanical illusion. And now the poor, dear little Daphne has died because of me."

The detective looked annoyed. He said, "Just what the hell are you trying to tell us, mister?"

"I come from the Mexican state of Yucatán," Sandrean explained. "There is the blood of proud and ancient peoples in me. The Mayans and the Toltecs and the Aztecs. They had a mighty god, the Feathered Serpent. Some knew him as Quetzalcoatl and others called him Kukulcán. When I produced his effigy I made a caricature of it for the amusement of the audience. I gave it a face as foolish as the face of the wooden dummy that my friend Montgomery uses in his act. I made it writhe and wriggle obscenely like a fan dancer. I caused the audience to hoot with laughter at my people's ancient god. And now death and murder have struck the house I live in."

Mrs. Mattingly dropped the role of Lady Macbeth and became the practical landlady again. "Oh, quit talking nonsense!" she said.

The pallid dancer, Elsa Travers, had come into the hall. She said, "It is not nonsense. Sandrean is right. There are many ancient mysteries we do not understand."

"You and your astrology and tea leaves and dream books," Mrs. Mattingly said disparagingly. "It's as silly to think that Sandrean's trick caused Daphne's death as it is for the police to believe James Lennox killed her."

Romano had come down the stairs. Bart nodded to him and started for the door. The policeman looked to Romano for confirmation before he let Bart pass.

There was a dim light burning now in the basement shop of the theatrical costumer. A man who wore a sports shirt and Bermuda shorts stood just inside the open doorway of the English basement. He was staring up curiously at the policeman at the door. He called to Bart, "Hey, mister! What happened in there tonight? I just saw them carry a body out."

On an impulse, Bart turned and descended the two steps to the shop. The man stood aside politely and motioned him inside. Bart walked through the door. The place was a confusion of colorful costumes of many periods of fashion. From the wall, huge carnival masks grimaced at Hardin.

Hardin said, "There was a murder upstairs tonight. Didn't you know that?"

"My God, no! They didn't kill old Mrs. Mattingly, did they?"

"A crippled girl was killed. A former dancer named Daphne Temple."

"That's awful," the shop proprietor said. "I knew the poor girl slightly. Saw her dance many a time before her accident. She was wonderful. Who killed her? Do they know?"

"They're trying to blame it on an old actor who works for me now. Jim Lennox. I'm Bart Hardin of the *Broadway*

Times, and old Jim has been acting as a kind of secretary for me."

The costumer said, "That's absurd. I know old Jim well. He wouldn't harm a fly. He comes down here often and we cut up touches about Broadway in the old days. Just the other night he put that big plumed hat over there on his head and gave me a scene from *Cyrano*. He's still got what it takes. By the way, my name is Trenchard. Dick Trenchard."

"Glad to know you," Bart said. "I hope that plume on the hat isn't a goose feather. It might make the cops more suspicious. They found goose feathers around the girl's body."

"Goose feather? Of course not. It's an ostrich plume. They're darned hard to come by nowadays."

"Has your shop been open all evening?" Bart asked. "I thought it was dark when I went by here a little while ago."

"It was," Trenchard said. "I worked tonight on a consignment for a summer theatre up in Sharon, Connecticut, but I locked up a little before ten o'clock. Then I remembered something I'd forgotten to put on the invoice. So I came back just a few minutes ago, just when they were taking the body out."

"Did you look outside at all while you were working here earlier?" Bart asked.

"I may have gone out for a breath of air a time or two. But I didn't see anybody until I was leaving at a few minutes to ten, I guess it was. I saw someone go in then. It was just one of the roomers, though. That dumpy little Mexican magician. He was all dressed up in evening clothes."

"Did you see him come out again?"

"No. I wasn't here. I saw him as I was closing up the shop."

Bart started for the door. He did not suggest that Trenchard inform the police of Sandrean's visit to the house.

"So long," Bart said over his shoulder as he left the shop.

He found a cab and directed the driver to Marty Land's private town house on East Sixtieth near Madison. It was after midnight now, but there was no trace of a breeze and the city was a great stone oven.

Bart knew the Broadway Mouthpiece would be in town. He was defending the sensational case of a young socialite playboy who had got himself mixed up in the call-girl business. There was no assurance Land would be home, of course. Marty was a rounder and a night owl.

Land's house was a narrow, elegant, three-storied structure

wedged in between two tall buildings. Marty's man, properly attired despite the heat and the hour, answered the doorbell. Bart gave his name and was relieved to learn that the attorney was home.

The servant ushered Bart into a high-ceilinged, air-conditioned living room. Knowing Land, Bart had expected the furnishings to be brashly contemporary. They weren't. The room was tastefully decorated with deep-piled rugs and traditional English pieces polished to a gleaming luster. Over the onyx mantel one of Blakelock's golden moons shimmered on dark water through a weeping-willow tree. Marty seemed to fancy dim and dolorous landscapes. He collected Blakelock and Innes, apparently. The crepuscular foliage of the paintings on the wall made this house in mid-Manhattan seem almost sylvan.

Land entered in a few moments, wearing shantung pajamas and a raw-silk robe. Even in dishabille he managed to appear elegantly poised. His face was handsomely sun-tanned, there were flecks of gray at his temples and his mustache was impeccably waxed. He said, "What's the matter, editor? One of your girl friends suing you for breach of promise at this time of night?"

Bart told him the story. When he finished, he fished for the crumpled bills he had thrust in his pocket when he left the crap game. He tossed the misshapen wad on a table. "There's about fifteen hundred there," he said. "Will it do for a retainer?"

"You're mighty careless with your money, carrying it like that," Marty commented. "Take it back. Bet it on a big horse when they open up at Saratoga. I don't want it."

"You won't take the case?"

"I took it as soon as I heard Jim Lennox's name," Marty declared. "He's one of the few men on Broadway I've ever admired. He's got a kind of goodness it's hard for guys like you and me to understand. So I'm going to pamper myself. I'm acting for him all the way, without fee. Oh, I'll get it back. I'll get it back the next time Selig sends one of his mobsters to me with a bum rap. I'll double his retainer. I'm kind of sore at Selig, anyway. He thought my prices were too high and he hired himself another boy. One of the goons the other boy defended just got burned in the Sing Sing death house, so Selig is sending me his business again."

Bart said, "Thanks, Marty, but I'd rather pay. This much, anyway. I won it in the floater."

"You can't pay," Land said with finality. "When Marty wants to pamper himself and make like a little tin angel he can afford the gesture."

Bart said, "For God's sake try to get the old man out of this as quickly as you can. He's got a heart condition and in this heat a jail cell may kill him."

"A heart condition? That's interesting. We'll pull the covers off a doc I know right away and get old Lennox examined and we'll have him sent to the city hospital instead of jail."

"A locked ward down at City will kill him just as fast as a cell in jail," Bart said.

"He won't be in any ward," Marty declared. "He'll have a private room with a cop standing guard at the door. When you get yourself suspected of murder, you get special privileges."

four

The fourteenth straight day of bone-baking heat and suffocating humidity had dawned. The weather forecast had become the only important news.

CITY SIZZLES AGAIN: NO RELIEF IN SIGHT, the bannerlines of newspapers screamed. Weather forecasters blamed it all on something called a Bermuda High that was lurking offshore and blocking the cool winds that might otherwise descend from the Canadian Rockies. The Bermuda High had become the villain in the piece, a great, squatting, immovable monster on a sit-down strike.

All over town rabid dogs were turning on their masters and men and women who had been happily married for a quarter of a century observed each other's beet-red faces and sweat-soaked bodies and suddenly knew loathing instead of love. The steaming corridors of hospitals were lined with beds for the heat prostration cases that were arriving hourly. Drugstores sold out of salt pills and a black market developed. Orders for air-conditioning units piled up so high that service men were six weeks behind schedule in installing them. The city parks that were usually closed to the public at midnight remained open and men and women threw their exhausted bodies down on the parched, dry grass.

Bart Hardin awakened in his bachelor flat above Bromberg's Flea Circus and Fun Arcade on Forty-second Street at an unusually early hour. At a little after eight o'clock he pulled himself to a sitting posture, reached for a bath towel he had flung on a nearby chair and wiped the crawling beads of sweat from his naked body. It wasn't only the heat that had kept him awake. His brief and troubled slumber had been haunted by the white face of an old man with dazed and pleading eyes.

Hardin's duties at the *Broadway Times* did not begin until noon, but he had things to do this morning and there was no possibility of further sleep, anyway. He let an ice-cold needle shower play over his body for ten minutes, then he shaved the pale blond stubble from his leather-brown jowls.

The Italian-silk suit he had worn the day before lay in a shapeless heap on the floor. He knew it would still be moist and he did not even bother to pick it up. He took an olive-drab poplin suit from the massive wardrobe and made a mental note that he was running short of lightweight clothes. He looked ruefully at a peacock assortment of embroidered vests that occupied most of the space in the wardrobe. Everyone on the Big Street sought desperately for a coat of arms, a symbol of his individuality in the bitter battle for recognition. In a cynical and, perhaps, a drunken moment, Hardin had chosen the riotously colored vests as his hallmark. It was too hot today for hallmarks.

Bart knew the shadowy stretches of the old-fashioned apartment would be far cooler than the street and he dreaded to leave, but he lingered only momentarily after he had dressed. He stood for a second tapping his fingers on the telephone, debating whether he should call Romano and tell him that Sandrean had returned to the house on Fifty-third Street between stage shows the night before. He decided against doing so. He and the swarthy lieutenant of police had been friends for many years, but now, suddenly, they were aligned on opposite sides, it seemed, because Romano was a cop.

Hardin clattered down the two flights of uncarpeted stairs and walked out into the furnace blast of Times Square. When he turned north on Broadway, the Big Street seemed almost eerie. There were queues of patient sufferers in the lobby of the Paramount and other picture houses, waiting to obtain the specially reduced prices for the morning show, to buy three hours of air-cooled comfort with the coins they clutched in sweaty palms, but the Big Street itself was virtually deserted. In the haze of heat the massive buildings that flaunted an electric alphabet of signs on their façades seemed to tilt at crazy, jigsaw angles, and as far as the eye could see Times Square resembled one of the painter Chirico's weird, unpeopled thoroughfares.

Near the corner where an enormous, electrically lighted waterfall plummeted down between two forty-foot pop bottles to advertise a cola drink, Hardin turned into a short-order restaurant called the Copper Skillet. For an undisciplined man who lived his life on a bedlam street, Hardin's habits were remarkably routine. He almost always ate his breakfast here, though he usually did not eat it until nearly noon. At this early hour the air conditioning had not begun to function properly and the atmosphere stank moistly of stale tobacco smoke and frying grease. Despite his lack of appetite and the heat and his state of mind, Hardin ate his usual breakfast of ham and eggs washed down with three cups of black coffee. Then he made his way to Fifty-third Street.

It was a little after nine-thirty when he rang the bell of Cora Mattingly's rooming house. A colored maid opened the door and presently Mrs. Mattingly appeared, looking ridiculously like a plump, flustered hen in her feathered silk negligee.

Bart said, "I wonder if Sandrean is home? I wanted to see him a minute."

Mrs. Mattingly called to the maid, who was busily swiping at the grandfather clock with a feather duster. "Did Mr. Sandrean go out for his breakfast, Dora?"

Dora shook her head. "I don't think so, ma'am," she said.

"He usually goes out for his breakfast around this time," Mrs. Mattingly explained to Bart. "His room's right at the top of the stairs on the third floor, the one just over James' little room, if you wish to go up."

Bart said, "Thanks. I will. And there's another thing. I'd like to take a look in the Temples' room, if I may."

Cora Mattingly hesitated. Then she said, "Will it help poor James if I let you go in there, Mr. Hardin?"

"It might," Bart answered.

"Then I'll unlock the door, but you mustn't tell on me and you mustn't disturb anything. The police made me promise to keep it locked, you see."

Bart said, "They'll never know I've been there."

Hardin walked up the two flights of stairs. He found the door of the magician's room had been left open for ventilation. The dumpy little Mexican was standing in front of a mirror adjusting the knot of a wildly colorful hand-painted necktie and perspiring profusely.

Hardin said, "Good morning."

The magician turned a startled moon-face to Bart. "Oh, Mr. Hardin!" he said. "I hardly expected a caller at such an early hour. Come in."

Bart went into the room and perched on the arm of a chair. Sandrean waited expectantly and Hardin let him wait before he spoke. Then he said suddenly, "Did you tell the police you came back to this house last night when you were supposed to be at the theatre?"

Sandrean froze, staring at himself in the mirror. "Who told you I came back here?" he asked.

"A man who saw you come into the house."

"Do the police know about it?"

Hardin said, "That's what I'm asking you."

Sandrean turned slowly toward Hardin. "I didn't tell the police," he said. "I didn't think it was important."

"It might have been important," Hardin told him. "A murder was committed here last night."

"But it had nothing to do with the murder. I came here an hour or more before the murder was committed. About ten minutes to ten, I think. And I left immediately. I had to leave immediately. The last stage show goes on at the Music Hall at ten o'clock and my own act is at twenty after. I had to draw it rather fine."

"Did you see anyone while you were here?" Bart asked.

Sandrean said, "The door to the Temples' room was open, for cross-ventilation, I suppose. It was very hot, of course. I tapped on the panel lightly, and when there was no answer I glanced inside to make sure Daphne was all right. She was sitting in her wheelchair, sleeping peacefully, an open book on her lap."

"Are you sure she was sleeping, that she wasn't already dead?"

"But that was an hour or more before she was killed, Mr. Hardin! And of course I'm sure. I could see her bosom rise and fall. A reading light was lit beside her. The house was very quiet. I could even hear her breathing."

"Did you see Jim Lennox?"

"No. I assumed then he had gone to the theatre. I had left a ticket for him. The door to his room was ajar, but it was dark. I did not glance in."

"Why did you come back here?" Hardin asked.

Sandrean's dusky face flushed. "I wish you wouldn't ask me that, Mr. Hardin. It's—it's embarrassing."

"If you don't answer me, you'll have to answer the police," Bart told the little magician.

"Oh, I hope I won't!" Sandrean exclaimed. "When you tell the police things, it gets into all the newspapers, and that would be horrible. Horrible! You see, it's a most personal matter, Mr. Hardin."

Hardin waited while the Mexican stood biting his lips and making up his mind.

"I'll tell you," he said at length, "but I hope you will respect my confidence. I do hope you will, sir. You see, I wear dentures."

"What's that got to do with your coming back?" Bart asked.

"Last night I dropped my dentures in my dressing room, Mr. Hardin, and I broke the plate. I had to go on in about forty-five minutes. I was already in tails and white tie for my performance and there was nothing to do but dash back here and get the other plate I always keep on hand in case of such an emergency. I hope this fact will not become public, Mr. Hardin. It might be most embarrassing to me professionally. Ridicule is not nice. And there is a certain young lady in the house to whom I am paying court. I should not like her to learn that I wear dentures. It seems—well, indelicate."

Hardin studied the little man a moment before he spoke. It was hard to believe that his consternation was not genuine. Finally Bart said, "I'll keep your secret unless it turns out I can help Jim Lennox by revealing it. I won't stop at anything to achieve that purpose."

"Oh, thank you, Mr. Hardin! Thank you!" the Mexican said, his voice breaking with gratitude and emotion.

"Did you really believe that stuff you were telling us last night?" Bart asked. "That this murder was the result of the curse of some ancient god?"

"In the stress of circumstance, a man reveals too much of his inner self, perhaps," Sandrean answered. "The news came as a horrible shock and I spoke out without considering the reaction of others. I am a trickster, Mr. Hardin, a magician, a man who manufactures miracles. Yet I come from a race of brooding, contemplative people and I have seen many things that cannot be explained by trickery or sleight-of-hand or by the laws of nature. With Shakespeare, I believe there are more things in heaven and earth than are dreamed of in our philosophy. I do not pretend that I have psychic powers, Mr. Hardin, but I do sincerely think I have a certain extrasensory perception. There is a bond between Miss Travers, the young lady that I mentioned, and myself in this. She is addicted to fortunetellers and mediums and astrologers, seeking to explain the things that have no explanation. When I fashioned the effigy that burlesqued the great god Kukulcán, the Feathered Serpent, I had a strange feeling, a premonition or a warning. When I broke my denture just before my act I thought it might be attributed to the vengeance of Kukulcán. I had held him up to ridicule and he would do the same to me by forcing me to go out before a packed house and try to go through my magician's patter without teeth in my mouth. But that was trivial. When I walked home and the dark act of murder confronted me, I thought that this was the real vengeance of an ancient god. You are a skeptic, Mr. Hardin. You think I am a fool. But you should delve into the ancient mysteries as I have, sir. There is power in the old gods yet."

Hardin shook his head and grinned. "I'm afraid I'll have to leave the old mysteries to magicians," he said. "The present ones are enough for me."

"Will you breakfast as my guest, Mr. Hardin?" Sandrean asked. "There is an air-cooled place around the corner that makes an excellent mushroom omelette. I am very fond of mushrooms. Good things often thrive in dark places, you know."

"Thanks, I've eaten," Hardin answered.

They walked down the stairs together. Mrs. Mattingly had kept her promise. The door of the Temples' room was ajar. Bart pretended he wished to use the bathroom as an excuse for lingering on the second floor.

When he was alone he went into the room where Daphne Temple had met her death. It was a very large room, at least twenty-five by eighteen feet, Bart judged. It had probably been the master bedroom when this place was a private house. Daphne's pathetically vacant wheelchair, with the bullet hole in its frame, stood beside a large, comfortable-looking bed. The other bed in the room was a day couch, against the opposite wall. It was snugly made, with a tailored corduroy spread, and with three square pillows, zippered into corduroy covers, to form a backrest.

Bart stood uncertainly in the room, not knowing just what he might be looking for. A brief breeze blew through the window on the fire escape and a small feather swirled across the carpet. The identification men had missed one of the goose feathers, Hardin thought.

A strident, nasal voice spoke suddenly behind him.

"Well, look who's here, Charlie! Mr. Hardin, the newsboy. Do you think he'd put our pictures in the paper? Do you, huh, Charlie?"

Bart turned and faced Charlie Montgomery, the ventriloquist. Montgomery's dummy was in his arms and the wooden jaws were still flapping. The dummy had a comic-character, red-nosed face and was dressed in hobo costume.

Montgomery said, "You're an impudent boy, Woodenhead Willie. You shouldn't ask Mr. Hardin a thing like that."

The dummy's jaws began to clack again. "I think Mr. Hardin's pretty dumb. Doesn't he know about things like fetishes and feathered serpents? Doesn't he know that little Elsa has a magician for a boy friend? Or is he stupid like those policemen who were here? Can't he figure out why poor Daphne was killed?"

Hardin had ceased to be amused, but Montgomery's puckish young face shone brightly as he said, "You musn't talk like that, Woodenhead Willie. After all, what have Elsa's boy friends got to do with poor Daphne's death?"

"You're a dumb cluck, too, Charlie," Woodenhead Willie snarled nasally. "Don't you know that Elsa's not in love with the magician? Don't you know she was in love with her dancing partner? So who'd be suspected if her dancing partner's wife was murdered? Why, poor Elsa, of course. And who would want a dirty thing like that, to make Elsa a murder suspect? Why, the magician scorned, of course. It's what you might call the Vengeance of the Feathered Serpent. At least that's what a certain screwball Mexican I know might call it."

"Shut up, Woodenhead Willie! You're talking nonsense!" Montgomery ordered sternly.

"Nonsense, huh?" Willie's jaws were flapping busily again. "That's the trouble with you humans. You don't know what nonsense is. You know, if Mr. Hardin would only turn around and look out that window in back of him, he'd see something right interesting."

Hardin turned. In the house next door a young woman was dressing and because of the heat she had not pulled the shades. She was clad only in panties and a bra.

"Ho, ho, ho!" chortled Woodenhead Willie. "Mr. Hardin is a naughty boy. Mr. Hardin is a Peeping Tom, that's what he is! But the really interesting thing is just to the right of where he's looking, in the wall beside the window."

Hardin finally spoke. "I don't see anything but a little hole in the wall," he said.

"How do you like that, Charlie?" Woodenhead Willie asked. "Mr. Hardin doesn't see anything but a hole in the wall! What do you suppose a guy like Sherlock Holmes or Sam Spade or Philo Vance would make out of a little hole like that?"

Montgomery's impudent face was suffused with mirth. He said to Hardin, "I'm really awfully sorry, you know. Willie's terribly garrulous and there's not a thing I can do to control him when he goes on one of his talking sprees. Don't pay a bit of attention to him."

Montgomery left the room chuckling, bearing Wooden-head Willie in his arms.

Hardin waited a minute. Then he walked to the window, leaned out and examined the hole in the wall more closely. The young woman pulled down her shade angrily. Bart left the room. He locked the door behind him and removed the key. He went downstairs and gave the key to Cora Mattingly. "Tell me," he said, "is there bad blood between Sandrean and young Montgomery?"

"Bad blood?" the landlady answered. "Why, no. Of course not. They're just friendly rivals, that's all. They've both been courting Elsa Travers."

Bart said, "I see," and bade good-by to Cora Mattingly. He walked to the office of the Broadway Times, an ancient building on Eighth Avenue near Fifty-first that had once been a fire house. When he was inside, the phone girl called to him.

"You sure get some screwy calls, Mr. Hardin," she said. "Take a look at this message I just wrote down for you."

Bart examined the slip of paper she handed him.

"Tell Mr. Hardin he will learn something to his advantage if he visits the Gypsy at the Romany Tearoom," it read.

five

Hardin read the message over again. Then he said to the phone girl, "Who gave you this message, Bertha? Do you know who it was that called?"

"I wouldn't know, Mr. Hardin," Bertha answered. "My God, it sounded like Sarah Bernhardt's ghost or something. Real scary-like, if you know what I mean." Bertha batted her false eyelashes and attempted to mimic the husky voice she had heard over the telephone. " 'Tell Mr. Hardin he will learn something to his advantage . . . ' " Her imitation of the ghost of Sarah Bernhardt was marred somewhat by her Brooklyn accent.

The phone girl looked up at Bart and fluttered her eyelashes provocatively, like Miss Marilyn Monroe registering emotion. "Do you believe in fortunetelling, Mr. Hardin? The horoscope in the *Daily News* now, that's my weakness. But once my sister over in Brooklyn had her fortune told at Coney and this Gypsy said she was going to meet a tall, dark man, and you know what? She met the guy she married, Herman, his name was, that very same day down on the beach. Only he wasn't tall and dark. He was short and red-headed."

Bart grinned at Bertha. " 'There are more things in heaven and earth, Horatio,' " he said.

"Who's Horatio?" Bertha called after him as he went into the city room.

Apparently Bertha hadn't read about the murder and Jim Lennox's involvement in it. Besides the horoscope she seldom read anything in the papers except stories that had the word sex in a headline. It was obvious from the curious faces turned toward him, as Hardin walked the length of the big editorial offices, that others had read of Lennox's plight.

Bart was early and only a few members of the staff had arrived. The enormous city room, which had housed fire engines and horses in the eighties, seemed deserted. Old Pops Taylor, the turf editor, sat in the slot of a horseshoe copy desk that curved around the brass pole the fire laddies had once coasted down. In a far corner a limp and elegant young man named Clayton Paulding was pecking at a typewriter, his long, slim fingers poised delicately above the machine before they descended to strike lightly on the keys. The rhythmic motions of his wrists made him seem more like a maestro conducting a symphony than a reporter batting out a story. Paulding was a protégé of Maddox Slade, who owned the *Broadway Times*. He wrote a very arty column he called "The Dance." Bart doubted that anyone except Maddox Slade and Paulding's mother ever read the column. Most of the dancers with whom the Broadway Times was concerned considered an off-to-Buffalo the height of artistic achievement.

Orville Cartwright, the six-foot, red-headed adolescent who was the copy boy, lumbered toward Hardin, his elephantine tread shaking the old floor boards. He addressed Bart with respectful concern. "Is Mr. Lennox going to be all right, Mr. Hardin? Is there anything I can do? Will they let you visit him in the hospital? Maybe I could take him down something to read. I've got a lot of very interesting pocketbooks back in the morgue."

Bart patted the boy's shoulder and said, "He's going to be all right, Orville. I'm going to see to that."

Hardin walked into the cubicle he called his office, switched on an electric fan, hung his coat on a clothes tree and loosened his collar. He was seating himself at his battered roll-top desk when Pops Taylor ambled in. Old Pops, who had served the *Broadway Times* for forty years, peered at Bart over half-moon glasses. "You ain't gonna let 'em electrocute old Jim, are you?" he asked. "Don't let 'em do that. He's the only man on earth who's older than I am. I don't want to be the oldest man on earth."

Bart said, "I've got Marty Land for him. That's about the best I can do until we catch the guy who really murdered her."

"It's got me all upset," Pops complained. "It's awful what they can do to an old man in this town. I've had to refer to Volume 9 three times already since I came to work."

Pops kept a complete set of the American Stud Book in a corner of the city room. He always had a whisky bottle stashed behind Volume 9.

As the old man turned to leave, Bart said, "Ask that Paulding to come in a minute, will you, Pops?"

"Okay," said Pops. "But what the hell you want with him? You taking dancing lessons?"

A minute or two later Paulding came into the little office,

moving with conscious grace. Despite the wilting heat he
appeared cool and fresh in close-fitting shantung slacks and
a sports shirt cut as full as a ballet dancer's waist. He said,
"You wanted me, Mr. Hardin?" He was the only person
on the staff besides the copy boy who addressed Bart as "Mr.
Hardin."

Bart said, "Yes. Did you read about the murder of this
dancer, Daphne Temple?"

"Yes. A terrible thing. I regret that your—your secretary
was involved."

"Never mind my secretary," Bart said. "Did you ever see
Adrian and Daphne dance? They called themselves the Temple Dancers, I believe. Or were they beneath your artistic
notice?"

"Why, of course I saw them!" Paulding exclaimed en-
thusiastically. "They were wonderful! Superb! At least the
girl Daphne was. She was a true artist, Mr. Hardin.
Adrian . . ." Paulding shrugged. "Well, let us say that Adrian
was just a dancer. He's been nothing since Daphne's accident.
A mere hoofer."

"Tell me something about them," Bart asked.

"I really didn't know them personally, of course. Only as
artists. They would be hard to classify under any of the usual
categories. I suppose 'satiric dancers,' the term we use for
that wonderful team, Mata and Hari, today, would be as
good as any. They were interpretive dancers in a sense. They
might be called 'storyline' dancers, if you will permit me to
coin a descriptive term."

Bart thought a minute, then he said, "Did any of their
dances have anything to do with ancient Mayans or Aztecs,
for instance?"

Paulding looked prettily puzzled. "No," he said. "I don't
think that would have been their dish of tea at all. They
didn't perform the classic or ritual dances, you know."

"I wouldn't know," said Bart. "I never saw them dance.
Tell me this, then. Did they use feathered costumes in any
of their dances?"

"But of course! They wore delightfully whimsical feathered
costumes in their very best number. It was called 'The Little
Goose,' and it was perfectly delightful in its conception. A
kind of travesty on the danse apache, told in terms of Aesop's
second fable. Instead of the Montmartre ruffian of the danse
apache, Adrian was dressed as a great, hulking gander.
Daphne didn't play the poor girl who has her torso tossed

around so casually by her lover. She played the little goose. Of course her costume was all feathers, head to foot. In this version, the little goose keeps trying to win the gander's love with presents like brightly colored Easter eggs. But the gander spurns them. He wants only a perfectly enormous golden egg that is the focal prop in the dance. Finally the little goose manages to carry the huge golden egg to the gander, but the effort is too much for her and she expires at his feet as the dance ends."

Paulding looked at Bart accusingly. "I did a long column about the Little Goose dance a few years ago," he said. "I always considered it one of my best pieces. I thought you might have remembered it."

"Sorry," Bart said. "It must have slipped my mind." He gave Paulding's columns to a long-suffering copyreader to whom the subject of a story was immaterial. The copyreader had done desk work so long that reporters' stories meant to him only a long series of misspelled words, misplaced punctuation marks and grammatical errors.

The phone on Bart's desk rang as Paulding left. Bertha announced that Marty Land wished to see Mr. Hardin. You could almost hear Bertha's false eyelashes rustling over the telephone. The suave and ingratiating attorney for the *Broadway Times* was outranked only by Marlon Brando in Bertha's gallery of heroes.

Marty walked briskly into the small office, smiling affably at Bart and exhibiting a perfect set of teeth. He was spruce in a suit of dark, nubby silk, but the carnation in his lapel had already begun to wilt. He hung a floppy-brimmed panama and a Malacca stick on the clothes tree and seated himself beside Hardin's desk. He touched his mustache tentatively. "This heat is hell on mustache wax," he declared. "Besides, you can't buy the good French wax any more. So few Americans grow mustaches it doesn't pay to import the stuff."

His keen eyes scrutinized Bart. He said, "I've done the best I could. Romano was cooperative and we've got Lennox in a private room down at City, certified as having a chronic heart condition. Maybe it would have been better in a ward, I don't know. It's an awfully small room and the heat is terrible. But at least he isn't lying next to the mumbling psychopaths and bloodstained brawlers they drag in from the streets. That's something."

"What about *habeas corpus?*" Bart asked. "We've got to get him out of there."

"Wrong move," Marty answered. "Worst we could make right now. If I ask for a writ I can probably get it because I know some obliging judges who owe Marty favors. But it would force the D.A.'s hand. Lennox isn't charged yet. He's just being held on suspicion. Once I flash a writ they'll bind him over to the grand jury for indictment. And they'll get it. It's about the tightest circumstantial case I've bucked in years. No. We play it cozy, like the guy who has his pair backed up in stud. Only we haven't got a pair backed up. It won't pay us to run a bluff right now, either. I'm afraid the old man just has to lie there and take it until Marty's agile little brain comes up with something smart."

"How is he, Marty?" Bart asked.

Marty said, "That's what I don't like. I got Doc Raines, a fine specialist, to examine him and to talk to the police medics. The heart's not too bad for a man his age. The blood pressure's up around 180. That's high, but a lot of men his age run that all the time and live to be a hundred. The thing is his mental state. He's practically in shock. Raines says that with heart cases the mental state can mean everything. And his is about as bad as it can get. There's not much medicine can do for him. The heat in that little room isn't helping, either. What we've got to do is get him out of there as soon as we can safely do so, and relieve his mind of the weight that's on it now. The only way to do that is find the person who murdered Daphne Temple."

Marty hitched up his trousers and crossed his slim legs. "I'm afraid that's your job, Hardin. You've played around at being detective before. You've helped to crack a couple of murder cases. The police won't be of much assistance because they think they've got the murderer. Romano has been as cooperative as possible. He says you've got a peeve on him, but you shouldn't have. He couldn't dodge taking Lennox in, and without Romano the old boy would be in a jail cell instead of a hospital. I had to have his help. He's given me all the leeway he can. He let me go to the psycho ward and talk to Adrian, even. Either this Adrian's a real mixed-up character or it's one hell of an act. He still says he killed his wife twenty-four hours before she died. Insists upon it, in fact. Also, he's scared to death they'll hurt him somehow."

Marty took a filter cigarette from a flat gold case and lit it. He blew smoke through his nostrils. "Romano even briefed me on the cops' end of it," he went on. "Ballistics showed there's no doubt the bullet that killed her was fired from the gun on the fire escape. There were no fingerprints on the gun. The autopsy showed just about what they expected. It confirmed the fact that she was probably killed just about the time the women heard the shot. The exact timing isn't possible, and it doesn't mean too much because the women heard the shot and the autopsy confirms the time they set as entirely reasonable. The feathers they found were goose feathers, according to the lab, if that's any help.

"If this was an ordinary case, I wouldn't worry a damn. I couldn't argue against the circumstantial evidence and I wouldn't try to. Actually, circumstantial evidence is the best evidence there is, but juries are always suspicious of it. I would hammer at the lack of motive and produce a whole stable of character witnesses to testify to Lennox's blameless life. Then I'd put the old man on the stand and let the jury get a good, long look at that aged-angel face of his and let him talk a little in that sweet old voice and it would all be over. Broderick, the D.A., couldn't find a jury that would convict. The trouble is, I don't think and Doc Raines doesn't think that he's ever going to live to face a jury if this thing drags out. We've got to get him out of it quicker than the red-tape of fair trial before his peers will allow. The only way to do that is to produce the murderer and clear him. That's your job, Hardin. I'll protect his legal interests, but the rest is up to you."

Bart said, "It's a big job, Marty. A terrible responsibility. I don't know if I'm up to it."

Land looked at Hardin's stricken face for a moment, then he chuckled. "Damned if this thing isn't almost funny in a way," he said. "If they took a poll on Broadway they'd probably vote you and me among the ten most hard-boiled guys on the street. You're a two-fisted drinking and gambling man who edits a blat that's not exactly a Sunday school paper. Both of us have avoided matrimonial shackles because we like to play the field with girls. I take money, a hell of a lot of money, from hoods like Selig for keeping their gunsels out of bum raps when the law moves in. They'd never invite either one of us to deliver an oration before the graduating class at Vassar. But we're both about to blubber and we're eating our damned hearts out because of an old man who has lived so innocently for seventy-five years it's doubtful that he ever learned the more interesting facts about the bees and flowers."

The phone on Bart's desk suddenly rang three shorts and one long. Phones all over the city room outside were doing the same thing. Orville Cartwright, the large young copy boy, had begun to parade up and down the city room, loudly whistling Sousa's "Stars and Stripes Forever."

"Oh-oh," Bart said. "The flags are up."

Marty Land's eloquent eyebrows asked a question.

"Maddox Slade, the owner of the Broadway Times has arrived," Bart explained. "He puts in a sudden and unannounced appearance on the average of three times a year and when he does there's usually something unpleasant on his mind. When royalty enters, Bertha warns us with a phone signal. Just in case somebody misses that, the copy boy starts whistling a Sousa march."

"Ah," said Marty. "Another of my esteemed clients. I hardly expected to see him today."

Slade, a distinguished-looking white-haired man, was already striding purposefully across the reaches of the city room toward Bart's cubicle. Orville had ceased whistling "The Stars and Stripes Forever." He was now standing stiffly at attention, like a West Pointer on dress parade. Paulding had rushed toward Slade at once and was greeting him obsequiously. Pops Taylor had been around too long to be impressed by newspaper owners. He was ambling over to consult Volume 9 again.

Slade came into the managing editor's office, nodded briefly to Bart. He stared hard at Marty, who had risen from his chair. "What are you doing here?" he demanded. "I hope the paper's not being sued for libel again."

"Don't worry, Maddox," Land said. "It happens that Hardin and I have mutual interests. His secretary is my client."

"Lennox?" asked Slade. "That's what I came down to see you about, Hardin. I don't like this business. I don't like it at all." Suddenly it dawned on him, and he turned to Marty. "You say you're representing Lennox? I won't have the paper's attorney representing him, Marty. That's out."

"I reserve the right to represent any clients I choose, Maddox," Land replied blandly.

"Not if you put their fees on the bill of the Broadway Times," said Slade. "Lennox is not even an employee of this paper. He's on Hardin's personal payroll. The paper isn't going to pay you a dime for defending him, Marty. Get that out of your head."

"I had no intention of charging his defense to your paper, Maddox."

"Then who's paying you? Old Lennox can't afford your fees. Hardin can't, either."

"I expect a man named Moe Selig to pay me eventually," Land said.

"That gangster? My God, don't tell me Lennox is mixed up with him! It's bad enough as it is."

"I doubt Lennox ever heard of Selig," Marty replied. "But Selig has a lot of money and I have a theory that men with lots of money should be philanthropic, even against their will. I'll simply add the cost of Lennox's case to one of Selig's accounts some day."

"Do you also add the cost of other people's cases to my account, Marty?"

Land gave Slade his genial, white-toothed smile. "If you find my fees too high, Maddox, I'll be glad to provide you with a Bar Association directory," he said. "Almost any name you choose would be a lawyer with lower fees than mine."

Slade prided himself on his poise under all circumstances. His usually pink face was crimson now and he was obviously fighting for self-control, but he could not resist another thrust.

"I can't say I like the idea of the attorney for this paper being associated with mobsters, either," he said.

"You are often associated with them yourself, Maddox," Marty answered amiably. "You invest a great deal of money in Broadway productions. Most of the productions couldn't get on the boards if men like Selig didn't invest money in them, too. They do it through dummies. Sometimes they even do it through me. I'm their front, you see. The only difference between you and me, Maddox, is that I admit the association and you pretend to be ignorant of it."

Slade was furious now, and he evidently did not trust himself to argue further with the lawyer. He turned to Hardin.

"I'll finally get to the point I came here to make, Hardin," he said. "It's this. This murder is a very nasty affair and the papers are associating the name of the *Broadway Times* with it. I don't like that. I want a page-one notice in the paper tonight to the effect that Lennox was not an employee of this paper, that he was nothing but the object of your own personal charity. I gave you a raise a while back in token of appreciation for certain services you had been able to render my wife and myself.* You chose to give the extra money to

* See *Shoot a Sitting Duck*, by David Alexander, Bantam Books, 1957.

this old man. I did not protest. You've been a soft touch for the bums and failures on the Street for years. Now this has backfired on you. I won't let it hurt the paper, too."

"No notice like that will appear in the *Broadway Times* while I am managing editor," Bart said flatly.

Slade bristled. He said, "I'm a lenient man, Hardin, and I hope I've been a considerate employer, but this is going a bit far. Are you refusing a direct order from me?"

Bart said, "I am. I'm refusing to prejudice the case of an innocent old man who is in enough trouble already. I refuse to break his heart by calling him an object of charity when he has been a useful employee to me and to this paper."

Slade started to speak, but Marty's smooth voice interrupted him. "Hardin is protecting your best interest, Maddox," he declared. "To publish such a statement would be a libel and a defamation. As your attorney, I advise against it."

Slade stood uncertainly for a moment. Then he said, "It seems my managing editor and my attorney are in league against me. I will have to give this matter serious thought. Maybe I *will* borrow that directory, Marty."

Land rose and got his hat and stick from the clothes tree. He took Slade by the arm and steered him toward the door. "Let me give you lunch, Maddox," he urged. "The chef at my club does trout with almonds and a wine sauce. It's a dish I'm sure you'll enjoy." He winked over his shoulder at Bart as he led Slade away.

Bart had no disposition to attack the copy and proofs in front of him after they had left. He glanced at the slip of paper Bertha had handed him.

He decided he would go and see the Gypsy.

six

The young intern at the city hospital was named Bell. He had not been out of medical school too long and he was not yet accustomed to being addressed as "Dr. Bell." He was an idealistic young man and at first the title of "Doctor" had seemed an accolade, but now he wondered if he would have gone through all the long years of study and privation to earn the right to print two letters of the alphabet after his name if he had known what the term of internship meant. He had once read a report from the American Medical Association that the average doctor earned the highest income of any professional man. It was right around $25,000 a year. That was more money than Bell had ever dreamed of making. But now he thought that this apprenticeship entitled doctors to every cent of it and more.

He was in a bad state at the moment. His white duck uniform was sickeningly moist and little rivulets of sweat stung his smooth, boyish face. The temperature in the old, overcrowded hospital was near 100 except in the air-conditioned inner offices of the more important administrators and Bell had little occasion to visit these comfortable precincts. He was nauseated and he kept his hands clasped into fists to prevent them from trembling. He told himself it was this awful unremitting heat. He couldn't afford to admit, even to himself, that it was just plain funk. Christ, he thought, how long are they going to keep me on the locked ward, catheterizing the filthy alcoholic derelicts who have reached the hopeless stage of wet-brain, how long am I going to have to listen to the fluttering heartbeats of the staring psychopaths who have already left the world and journeyed off into the dim and dreadful country of the insane? He pitied them, that was the trouble. A physician could not afford the luxury of pity. Bell had fought hard against his softness. The only way to protect himself from pity was to build a shell of hate, to hate them for their hopelessness, for the unmentionable things they did when nights were dark. But he could not really hate them. That was his weakness. The nurses regarded him as

46

competent but they disliked him because he was brusque and hard and unfeeling. Bell couldn't afford to reveal his feelings. That would have been fatal for him, would have ended his career before it was begun.

They had called him off the locked ward to attend a young girl who had been attacked the night before in a city park by a gang of six sadistic young hoodlums. She was dying. She was going to die very soon. Thank God for that, Bell thought. She's going to die this afternoon. If it had been left to him he would have practiced euthanasia to save her the torment of the few hours that were left. The girl was the age of his young sister.

And now he had to see the old man in the private room where the cop was standing guard. The old murderer. A particularly nasty old murderer. He had killed a young girl, too. A girl who was crippled from the hips down, who couldn't even try to run away when he attacked her. He must have killed her to silence her, to keep her from telling of the things that came into the old man's twisted, senile mind when he found the girl alone and helpless.

A policeman wearing a gun sat in a straight chair propped against the wall beside the door of the little private room. The policeman's blue shirt was black with sweat. He let the chair drop forward with a small crash as the doctor nodded to him. Without rising, he reached out and turned the key in the door. "Okay, Doc," he said.

The room was so small that the tilted hospital bed almost filled it. It was the most horribly hot place that Bell had entered during his tour of duty, which had begun early that morning. There was a large window by the bed, but it faced a blank brick wall. A steamy, grease-laden stench arose from the kitchens that were directly beneath the little room.

It was a child's figure on the bed, so small and wispy it seemed completely lost in the voluminous hospital gown. The old face that stared up at him was as innocent as a child's too. Bell steeled himself. *I mustn't pity him, I mustn't pity him.* As a medical man, Bell didn't like the staring eyes. There was the beginning of shock, of coma, of death in them. His experience told him that the old man wasn't going to last long in this hot and airless little room.

Bell hooked the stethoscope into his ears and listened to the old man's chest. Not too bad. A heart murmur, of course, but it wasn't that which was going to kill him. Bell wrapped the rubber bandage around the old man's arm and noted the diastolic and systolic pressures. Not normal, of course, but not too alarming, either. It was the thing which caused the look in the old man's eyes that was going to kill him. The old man's mind was abandoning the will to live. Even in his brief experience, Bell had seen it too many times to be mistaken.

As he held his fingers against the blue veins of the old man's wrist to take his pulse, Bell said, "How do you feel?" It was conventional for the doctor to say something to a patient, even though the patient had murdered a young girl about his sister's age.

The old man's defeated eyes, the eyes that held death in them, turned toward the young doctor. His voice was feeble when he spoke.

"I—I wonder if I could have an ice bag? My head is so awfully hot."

Bell released the old man's wrist suddenly. His fingers on the pulse had begun to tremble violently. He waited a moment to control his voice before he spoke. "The hospital's very short of ice in this weather," he said curtly. "We can't waste it just to cool your fevered brow. You're all right."

He got up and started for the door. He could feel the old man's eyes staring at his back. Suddenly he went to pieces completely. He turned savagely and cried, "Why did you do it? Why is an old man with a face like yours a degenerate murderer? Why? Why?"

The door opened and the policeman looked in.

"Is something wrong, Doc?" he asked.

"Yes," Bell answered. "Everything is wrong. Everything in the whole damned cockeyed world is wrong."

He hurried past the policeman and fled from the room.

The policeman closed the door again and locked it.

James Lennox turned over and buried his face in the wet pillow.

His slight body shook with silent sobbing.

seven

The Romany Tearoom was an upstairs mitt joint above a bowling alley on Eighth Avenue near Forty-eighth Street. Hardin had seen its gaudy sign many times on his way from the Sligo Slasher's bar to his flat above the flea circus. As he walked the four blocks from his office the noon-hour temperature had risen officially to 98.2, an all-time record for the date, and that temperature was taken on a breeze-swept roof that overlooked the Battery. Street thermometers were registering seven degrees higher.

There is a city ordinance against fortunetelling in New York, but like most laws it has loopholes. The fortunetellers, many of them real Gypsies, worked in the so-called tearooms, where tea-leaf readings were offered as a bonus to those who ordered the seventy-five-cent table d'hôte. If the customer appeared to be a real mark, he might be persuaded to pay a sub-rosa fee for a more comprehensive analysis of his destiny by a palmist or crystal-gazer in the back room.

Bart climbed a flight of uncarpeted stairs and entered the tearoom. It was narrow and dreary and suffocatingly hot. Dyed cheesecloth covered the walls and in this heat the faded mauve and burnt-orange hues were particularly sickening. Only a very few office girls had forgone the lunch-hour comfort of air conditioning in the hope that the dregs in their cups would reveal a muscular swain waiting to embrace them.

A bedraggled, red-haired waitress who reminded Bart of a wilted carrot approached and said, "Take any table you like, sir." The hopeful, perspiring office girls who were waiting to have their orange-pekoe analysis looked up at him curiously. Not many men came to this place.

Bart said to the waitress, "I want to see the Gypsy."

"She's busy right now, sir. But if you'll order, she'll read your leaves as soon as you've finished your tea," the wilted carrot assured him.

"Tell the Gypsy Bart Hardin is here."

"Oh. Are you a friend of Miss Alma's?" the waitress asked.

"Maybe you'd better ask Alma that," Bart replied.

The girl went toward the rear and pushed open a curtain.

Presently the Gypsy came through the curtain, warmly attired in drippy layers of cloth and wearing a scarf around her head.

She didn't look at all like a Gypsy except for her costume. Her face was pale and plump and the wispy hair that showed beneath the scarf was gray. The effect of the Romany costume was further impaired by the rimless glasses she wore over keen, intelligent brown eyes.

She said to Bart, "Mr. Hardin, you don't know me, I'm sure, but we met once a long time ago. James Lennox introduced us. I'd like to have a talk with you. Would you come into my office? I'm sure you wouldn't want to eat here. The cook's idea of solid nourishment is tuna-fish salad."

She led Hardin through the curtain to an airless closet that had apparently been a pantry at one time. There was a table covered by a sleazy piece of black velvet and a small crystal ball in the center of it. Charts with the mystic symbols of palmistry, phrenology and the zodiac hung on the wall.

The Gypsy said, "I'm Alma Turner, Mr. Hardin. I used to be an actress. Now I'm in a racket. It isn't a very vicious racket, though, and it's not profitable enough for the mobs to try to muscle in or the police to bother us too much. Maybe I even spread around a little sunshine in my own small way. These poor shopgirls and stenographers who come here don't have very much to brighten their lives. I always manage to see wonderful things for them in the leaves, handsome strangers and money and motor cars and ocean trips. It helps them to hope, and hope is good for people. The ones who want to spend a dollar or two more to have their fortunes told by the cards or have their palms read get their money's worth. They're starved for romance, mostly, and I supply it to the poor little things. It's not hard to tell them what they want to hear. I simply read the movie magazines and keep track of the current male heartthrobs. All I need to do is figure out if my client is the Rock Hudson or Tony Curtis type, so I'll see the right handsome stranger in the cards or in their palms or in the crystal ball. A little while later they meet some scrawny little guy at a dance hall and they think my prophecy has come true and they're happy. It's not wrong to make people happy."

Alma Turner laughed heartily. "There," she said. "It seems I almost always have to justify myself. Now that's over I'll get down to business. I was in the theatre for many years before I opened this tearoom. I played with James Lennox often. He was one of the finest men I ever knew. Once, years ago, when I was a stage-struck kid just starting out, he gave me a helping hand, and I've never forgotten it. I'm all broken up over this thing I've read about in the papers, this awful thing that's happened to him. And I know something that might help."

"What?" Hardin asked.

"I called you because I know how fond you are of Jim, how he works for you. I didn't think the cops would pay much attention to me. Besides, in my business I'm kind of allergic to cops. I suppose there's a law against what I do, but an old actress who can't get parts any more has to do something. Anyway, I thought I'd tell you instead of the cops. That girl who's connected with this case is crazy. Plumb crazy. I know her well."

"What girl?"

"That dancer who works with Adrian Temple. Elsa Travers is her name. She comes here all the time. That's the main trouble with this business, you attract a few psychos, and I'm a normal, healthy old gal who doesn't want any truck with them. Most of the kids who come here just want to hear that something wonderful is going to happen to them. I tell them it is, and they go away with a rosy glow, and that's all there is to it. But this Elsa woman is different. She's an odd-ball. She takes this psychic stuff seriously. She thinks a nice, simple old lady like me can pull apart the veils of the future and tell her what's going to happen on a certain date five or ten years from now. I've tried to brush her off, but I can't. She's like a religious fanatic. And all fanatics are dangerous people. I think this girl is entirely capable of committing murder, Mr. Hardin."

"Maybe so," Hardin agreed. "But you haven't given me much to go on."

"There's more than my opinion. She insists on talking to me, telling me all about herself. She's crazy in love with this drunken Temple. She had reason enough to want his wife dead. She used to bring Temple up here once in a while in the afternoons. I suppose it was a convenient rendezvous where they wouldn't run into anyone they knew. They were here together drinking tea for an hour or more a few days before the girl was killed. I was reading leaves at a nearby table and I couldn't help overhearing snatches of their conversation. It was intriguing, something about a feathered serpent. Apparently the serpent had something to do with the performance of a magician friend of theirs they'd seen the night before."

She looked at Bart. She said, "You're not too impressed, are you? I suppose it's really no help at all. But I just felt I had to try and do something for Jim Lennox. I love that old man because he's a genuine human being and he helped me when I needed help the most. I'm sure that girl is a weirdy, Mr. Hardin. I hope to God I'm not selling myself on my psychic powers, but I repeat I'm sure she's capable of murder. All fanatics are. There's no such thing as a harmless lunatic in my book. And she had a motive. About the strongest motive there is. She was in love with that dead girl's husband."

The wilted carrot thrust her head through the curtains. "The young ladies at table three are all upset because you haven't read their leaves, Miss Alma," she said.

Alma rose. "I'll be right out," she said. She turned to Bart. "Those two will be easy. I had a look at them. They're both Rock Hudson types. I'm sorry if I've wasted your time. I had to make a try."

Bart said, "The things you've told me may be helpful. I'll think them over and I'll keep in touch with you."

"Do that," said Alma. She chuckled. "And if you ever begin to feel that vague depression, come around and drink some tea. I'll conjure up a Gina Lollobrigida for you."

Hardin walked back to the *Broadway Times* office. The heat had made him about as physically uncomfortable as it was possible to get, and his mind was in a turmoil, but he attacked the copy and proofs that were piled in front of him. Perspiration dripped off his forehead and smeared the printer's ink on proofs and blotched the rough gray copy paper. The fat black pencil kept slipping in his sweaty hand. But he forced himself to work steadily. By four o'clock the first rush was over.

At four Hardin usually took a break and had his first drink of the day at the Sligo Slasher's bar across from the Garden. He felt guilty about going there this afternoon. He wanted desperately to do something to help Lennox, to devote all his spare time to trying to clear the old man's name. He could think of nothing he could do right now. He decided that there was no reason to interrupt his usual routine.

Tony Maclaren, the Sligo Slasher, had recently installed an air-conditioner on his premises, but it baffled the little man completely. As Bart entered the place a blast of hot, moist air and Maclaren's curses greeted him. Maclaren was a bantam rooster of a man who wore a silk shirt and a violent necktie and sleeve garters. He was twisting dials and kicking the machine and berating his purchase with the choicest oaths of Ireland. "It's a gyp!" he bellowed. "It's a quadruple gyp!"

Bart walked over and watched Maclaren's frantic efforts to force the cooling mechanism into operation. Finally he leaned over and turned a switch. There was a rattling noise and cool air began to flow from the gratings.

"There's nothing the matter except you turned it off," Bart said.

Hardin was working on his first glass of Irish on the rocks, when Eddie O'Grady, the Old Top Sarge, came bustling in. His open-throated sports shirt revealed the Congressional Medal of Honor that he habitually wore on a star-spangled ribbon about his neck.

The Old Sarge, who served Moe Selig as lookout and errand boy, said, "I knew I'd find you here around four, Captain. Moe Selig wants to see you. He says to tell you he's got some real Irish and an air-conditioner that works."

Hardin was puzzled. He could think of no reason the Broadway mobster should want to see him. Selig operated a loan-shark business as well as gambling enterprises and Bart had often borrowed sums from him at six-for-five interest, but at the moment he was solvent and owed Selig nothing. He said to the Old Sarge, "What does he want to see me about?"

"I wouldn't know, Captain. Moe Selig don't tell me his business. He just gives me orders. I got orders to bring you over."

Bart said, "Okay. I'll go." He finished the Irish in his glass and left the Slasher's with the old soldier.

Selig's place was half a block away, just east of Eighth on the stretch of Forty-ninth Street called Jacobs Beach by the Garden sports crowd. Selig's headquarters were innocuous enough from the outside. A cigar store was the front for the biggest of New York's horse rooms. The Old Sarge led Bart through the deserted cigar store with its dummy cigarette cartons and cigar boxes and pressed a buzzer. A heavy door opened.

The biggest bettors in New York assembled in this room. There was elaborate apparatus for receiving race results and the place was pleasantly cool. The Old Sarge led Hardin through the room and tapped on the door of Selig's private office. A buzzing sound announced that the lock was being released. Hardin pushed open the door and entered.

Selig's simian figure was seated behind a big desk. There was a stack of newspapers on the desk.

Seling grinned, said, "Hello, editor. Park it in a chair. I got an Irish all poured out for you."

Bart sat down and accepted the drink. He said, "What did you want with me, Selig?"

Selig waved his hand toward the pile of newspapers. "I been reading the blats," he said.

Bart waited.

Selig said, "That old pappy guy you stake has got himself a mess of grief. It's a funny thing. I never really met the character but I kind of like him. When I was a little kid I used to sit in the peanut roost at the Broadway shows when I could steal something and sell it. I saw that old man act when I was just a punk and I always remembered him. He was kind of like my old man. My old man wasn't worth a damn. He never knew what the score was and he never made a dime. But he was gentle, like this Lennox character. He liked to sit around and play the violin. He wasn't worth a good goddamn, but he was gentle."

Bart still waited.

Selig said, "Editor, I been around the Big Street more than thirty years. In all that time I kept my nose clean. But I'm going to do something I never did before. I think the heat has got me."

"What?" asked Bart.

"I'm going to stool, editor. I'm going to sing like a canary."

Hardin could think of no very good rejoinder to that.

"I hate to see this old pappy guy take a bum rap. I don't know why, but I do. And I've got some information that might be real useful if you play it right."

"What?" asked Hardin.

"There's a dame named Travers connected with this thing. Lives in the house where this crippled girl was chilled, according to the blats. Before she started dancing with this Temple guy she was a hoofer in the line at Benny Speakman's club, the Seventh Veil. While she was a hoofer there she bought herself a big, fat forty-five."

Moe drummed fingers on his desk. "I don't know why the hell I'm doing this," he said. "Maybe I should see a bug doctor. It's funny what remembering a little guy on stage and another little guy who used to sit around and play a fiddle can do to you. Anyway, there's a bouncer over at Benny's place named Stony Martin. You remember him? He used to be a fighter."

"He was a bum," Hardin said.

Selig chuckled. "He was right useful to the Syndicate in his fighting days," he said. "He was a stumble-bum for a lot of the champs who was coming up and he always remembered to dive in just the round the betting said he should. His brains got kind of scrambled up from taking Sunday punches. The boys were afraid he wouldn't remember to dive at the right time any more, so they had to retire him from the ring and take care of him. He's had some bouncers' jobs, but he's got another dodge. He used to work the longshore before he got to be a fighter. All the dock wallopers know him. When they're able to steal a little here and there they let Stony fence it for them. Mostly, Stony fences hot guns. A lot of them get lifted out of army shipments. Stony got hold of a batch of army forty-fives about two months ago. He sold us all we needed and he had some left. He sold one of them to this chick Elsa Travers, who was working at the club. I know, because we make Stony give us the names of all the people he sells hot goods to. It wouldn't do to let them get in the hands of the wrong parties. Somebody who might want to take a pot at me, for instance."

Selig leaned back in his chair. "That's it, editor. Now I've suddenly forgot that you were here. If somebody saw you come in, you just dropped around to make a bet in the horse room. And there's no use in trying to work on Stony. He's caught so many punches he wouldn't even feel a rubber hose. He won't talk. If anybody asks me, I'll say you've taken the pipe and are making up a story to try to save the skin of this old pappy guy. You can't expect me or Stony or anybody else to admit it to the cops or to take a witness stand. But you got some information now. Maybe you can figure a way of using it."

Hardin rose, said, "Thanks, Selig. I mean that."

As Bart was leaving, Selig called after him, "Hey, editor! What the hell you reckon made me do a thing like that?"

Bart grinned at Selig. "Maybe you're getting to be a real nice man," he said.

eight

Hardin's routine called for him to dine on steak at the Saddle and Whip Café on Broadway between seven and eight, after he had put the paper to bed and marked the first-run sample copies for correction and replate. Today his routine was considerably upset. He had breakfasted in the early morning, and despite the heat he was starved by the time the old press in the basement of the *Broadway Times* made the ancient building shake with earthquake spasms. He did not go directly to the Broadway restaurant, however. He walked south on Eighth Avenue and again climbed the stairs to the Romany Tearoom.

The place was still open, but it was completely deserted. Alma Turner came out of the little office, dressed now in flowery voile, and she resembled a well-to-do Westchester grandmother more than a gypsy fortuneteller. She met Hardin in the dimly lighted premises and said, "Mr. Hardin! We're closing up. We had absolutely nobody here for dinner, and I can't blame them for staying away since we don't have air conditioning. Usually we stay open to catch the girls after the picture houses let out, but not tonight. I'm letting the help off early and I'm leaving myself. I can't stand the heat in that little pantry I call an office any longer."

Hardin said, "Do you think you could stay just a little longer, maybe?"

"Don't tell me you want to eat here, Mr. Hardin! I assure you the food is simply lousy. You can't serve decent food today at the prices I charge. The cook has already left and the waitress is back getting dressed."

"It might be better if you were here alone," Hardin said. "I want you to do something for Jim Lennox."

Alma nodded readily. "I'll stay," she said. "I'll do anything to help old Jim. Just tell me what I have to do."

"Do you think you could get Elsa Travers to come down here tonight?" Bart asked.

"I've had a hard time keeping her away in the past," Alma answered. "Why do you want her here?"

She motioned Hardin to a small table. He sat down and she

56

took the chair opposite him. She switched on the fringed table lamp. The waitress came through from the rear, dressed for the street. She said, "Good night, Miss Alma."

Alma bade her good night. She smiled at Bart, said, "Now let's act like conspirators. We're all alone. I think I kind of like this, you know."

"I'd like you to call Elsa Travers. I want you to tell her that you've seen something in the cards or in your crystal ball or maybe that you've summoned up the spirit of her great-grand-father. Tell her you think she is in great danger and you want to warn her. Tell her you think she should come down for a reading or whatever you call it right away. Do you think that would get her here?"

"She'll run all the way, even in this heat," Alma assured him. 'I've told you she's unbalanced. She's a fanatic on this occult stuff. But what do I do when she gets here?"

"Read her palm or tell her fortune with cards or look at her tea leaves. Whatever you think is most impressive. Tell her you see a gallows as a symbol of her destiny."

"I'm beginning to love this," said Alma Turner happily.

"Tell her there are two men in her life who are very dangerous to her. One is a man who has some relation to a stone or a rock. Maybe his name is Stone or maybe he's nicknamed Rocky."

"Wait a minute," said Alma, reaching for an order pad and pencil. "Maybe I'd better make some notes."

She scribbled on the pad as Bart went on. "Describe this man as being muscular and violent and having a battered face. You might go so far as to tell her he has some connection with a night club where she has worked. Then tell her there is another man who knows about her relation with the first one and that this places her in grave danger. Describe this second man as me. Make him as ugly as you want, but be sure she recognizes him, that's the important part."

"You're not hard to describe, Mr. Hardin. That pale blond hair and dark bronze skin is a distinctive combination. And your nose is a little out of shape, as if it had been broken."

Bart said, "It was. In the Golden Gloves a long time ago."

"What next?" Alma asked.

"That's all."

"But what happens? What do you expect her to do?"

"I don't really know. I want to see what she'll do. That's the interesting part. That's the thing that may help Jim Lennox."

"I'll call her right away," Alma said. "Do you have her number?"

Bart took a notebook from his pocket. Because Lennox worked for him, he had jotted down the number of Cora Mattingly's rooming house. He gave the number to Alma Turner.

Alma went to a coin telephone near the door of the tearoom. She was gone for several minutes. When she returned, she nodded. "She was home. I told her enough to get her here on the run. I was almost ashamed of myself for laying it on so thick. She'll be flying through that door any minute now."

"Good work," Bart said. "I'll be shoving off now. I'd like to call you in a couple of hours and find out her reaction. Where can you be reached?"

Alma wrote a number on the order pad. "That's the telephone," she said. "I live in a small women's hotel on Twenty-ninth, near the Little Church Around the Corner."

Bart left the tearoom and walked to the Saddle and Whip for his delayed dinner. There were people on Broadway, a lot of them, but the crowds were sparse for this hour of the evening and those who walked the Street moved slowly in the heat, like zombies in a daze. There were lines at the air-cooled theatres and the refrigerated barrooms were packed. One moppet of six or seven was protesting vociferously against his mother's admonitions to remove his Davy Crockett fur cap despite the sizzling heat.

It was after nine when Hardin finished his coffee and paid his check. He walked through the Big Street's haze of heat to Cora Mattingly's old-fashioned rooming house on Fifty-third. The landlady informed him that Elsa Travers had received a phone call and had left in a great hurry an hour before and had not returned.

Bart said, "Did you check the furnishings of the Temples' room after the murder, Mrs. Mattingly? Was there anything missing?"

Cora looked puzzled. "Why, yes," she said. "The police asked me to do that. There was nothing missing."

"Are you sure a bed pillow wasn't missing?"

"How strange that you should ask that!" Cora exclaimed. "No, there wasn't a bed pillow missing from the Temples' room, but a pillow was missing from the linen closet today when Dora, the maid, went over the house supplies. It was a brand-new pillow that has never been used. I was saving it for my daughter's room when she returns from her engagement in

Louisville. It was a good pillow, one I just bought the other
day at a sale at Macy's. It was filled with goose feathers and
goose down. That sort of pillow is very expensive. The other
pillows in the house are stuffed with chicken feathers. And it
was the funniest thing. There was another pillow in the closet
that I'd never seen before. It was a cheap pillow filled with
kapok."

Bart said, "That's very interesting."

"It's very upsetting to me," Mrs. Mattingly replied. "In
all the time I've operated this house there's never been such
a thing as this petty pilferage. I've tried to run it like the old-
fashioned theatrical lodgings, where the roomers were one big
family who could live together in mutual trust. I don't like
this a little bit, Mr. Hardin."

"I don't like it too much, either," Bart told her. "It sort
of upsets a pet theory of mine. I wonder if I could have another look at the Temples' room, Mrs. Mattingly?"

Cora Mattingly hesitated. "I really shouldn't let you," she
said. "I did promise the police and I'm a woman who usually
keeps her word. But I am so distressed about poor James. If
your going in the room can help him any, I'll let you. Only
you must leave everything just as you find it."

"I only want to climb out on the fire escape and look at the
house next door," Bart said.

The plump woman sniffed. "Oh," she said stiffly. "I think
I understand. There seems to be quite an attraction in the
house next door in this weather when everyone leaves their
windows open. Mr. Sandrean and Mr. Montgomery live right
above and they've been enjoying the view, too."

Bart grinned. "Believe me, that's not it," he said. "There's
a hole in the wall I want to look at."

"All right. But you must promise you will stay only a few
minutes. I wouldn't want the police to come here and find
I'd broken my word."

Bart reassured her. They walked upstairs and she unlocked
the door to the Temples' room. Bart switched on the light
and crossed to the window on the fire escape. The young
woman next door still had her shade up and she was as scantily
attired as before. She seemed to be a dancer. She was standing
in front of a mirror in her brief costume of panties and bra,
stretching one well-shaped leg out behind her and balancing
on the other. Bart climbed out on the fire escape. He leaned
over the railing. The wall of the next house was lighted by the
glow from the two windows. It was about six feet across, Bart

judged. He could see the little hole in the wall quite clearly.

The blonde young woman next door discovered Bart. She walked to the window and stared hard at him. Then she went to the other side of the room, put on a smock and returned to the window. The gesture of donning the smock wasn't quite as modest as it appeared. She forgot to button the smock and it concealed very little. She looked at Bart a moment, then she said, "Hey, mister, what are you doing out there? Are you a cop or are you just a nasty man?"

"I'm not a cop and I hope I'm not too nasty," Bart replied. "I'm a newspaperman."

"Oh, yeah? What are you doing out on somebody else's fire escape? You don't live there, do you? Isn't that the room where the murder was committed?"

Bart said, "That's right. I'm just snooping around. All newspapermen snoop around. That's the way they make their living."

"What paper are you with?" the blonde asked. "One of the tabs?"

"I'm managing editor of the *Broadway Times*," Bart told her.

"The *Broadway Times*? Hey, that's show business. I've been trying to get a break in that rag for years."

Bart said, "Were you home last night when the girl was killed?"

The girl shook her long yellow bob. "Uh-uh. I got a specialty spot in a club out on the Island last night. A girl got taken with the heat. But she got well again real quick, so I'm out of work again tonight."

Her youthful face studied Bart. She said, "You really on the *Broadway Times*? Why couldn't you run a little story about me, or a picture, maybe? I've got some poses that would sell a million copies."

"Why don't you let me come over and we'll talk about it?" Bart suggested.

The girl played coy. "Well, I don't know . . ."

"What bell do I ring?"

The girl said, "Apartment 24. The name's Chloe Fields."

"Mine's Bart Hardin. I'll be right over."   .

He climbed back into the room, switched off the light. He closed the door and locked it. Downstairs, he gave the key to Cora Mattingly. She told him that Elsa Travers had not yet returned.

The house next door was a large building that had been

cut up into small apartments. Bart found Chloe Fields' bell in
the corridor and a buzzer released a heavy door. There was a
self-service elevator, but Bart mounted the stairs to the second floor. Chloe awaited him, with her door partly opened,
peeping out. She had not buttoned the smock.

Bart said, "Hello, sugar. You look nice and cool."

The girl said, "I'm not cool, but I don't mind the heat too
much. I'm used to it. I come from a little town in Georgia."

She ushered him into a one-room studio apartment that
was the exact duplicate of a million other one-room studio
apartments in New York City.

Chloe said, "I can make you some gin and tonic. It's a
good hot-weather drink."

Bart shook his head, "About all I drink is Irish whisky. But
make yourself one. Maybe I can chew on the ice cube."

The girl shook her long bob at him. "You're particular,"
she said. "You know what I really like? Corn whisky. Plain old
white mule like we have down home. You can't get it up
here."

She took a sheaf of photographs from the day bed. "I got
these out while you were coming over," she said. "Some of
them are pretty good." Bart glanced at them. In the photographs Chloe wore some rudimentary garments, but they were
about the size of the loop earrings that dangled above her
rounded shoulders and they covered just about as much anat-
omy.

Bart said, "They're real pretty, sugar. I'll look them over in
a minute, but there's something I want to do first."

"You mean the little boys' room? It's that door on the left."

Bart crossed the room, said, "I want to look out this window."

"Jeez," said Chloe. "I never saw a man who was so queer
for windows."

Bart twisted a gooseneck lamp on the desk so that it shone
out the window on the hole in the wall. He sat straddled on
the window sill and leaned out. He took a penknife from his
pocket and began to chisel around the edges of the small hole.

Chloe regarded him with her hands on her hips. "You're
the first guy who ever came in here just to sit on my window
sill," she said.

After a little while, Bart extracted a small pellet from the
hole and dropped it in his pocket. "What's that, honey?"
Chloe asked.

"A luck piece, maybe," Bart said.

Chloe came close to him as he walked away from the window. She stood invitingly in front of him. The open smock had slipped down off her shoulders. "This could be your lucky night," she said. "You know, you're a right attractive fellow, even with that funny busted nose." She teetered closer to Bart and put a hand caressingly on his arm. "I need some publicity awful bad," she said. "Things are rough at this time of year. Why don't we sit down on the couch and see how you like my pictures?"

Bart said, "May I ask you something?"

The girl's young face looked up at Hardin provocatively and she chuckled. "Lots of fellows ask me something," she replied. "I don't bite, honey. Go right ahead. What do you want to ask?"

"Can I use your phone?" said Bart.

The girl shoved his shoulders and turned her back on him. "Oh, sure," she said. "Use the phone. You want to tell your mother you'll be home late?"

"I want to call the cops," Bart answered, picking up the phone and dialing Manhattan West.

The girl swung her body around quickly and glared furiously at Bart. "Say, who the hell are you, mister? A fly cop on the vice squad? I'm a dancer and I've got a chorus Equity card to prove it!"

"I'm calling Homicide," Bart answered. "I want a certain cop I know to come up here and see that hole in your wall and look at the little luck piece I dug out of it."

Bart got Romano on the line. The lieutenant agreed to come up to Miss Fields' apartment.

While they were awaiting the detective's arrival, Bart said, "Maybe you'd better button up that smock before the lieutenant gets here, sugar. He's an Italian and you know that Latin temperament."

"Gee," said Chloe, slowly buttoning the smock. "This started out to be a real nice evening."

They spent the few minutes before Romano arrived looking at the photographs. Bart had to admit there was a lot to look at.

Romano and Grierson took about twenty minutes to reach Fifty-third Street. Young Grierson had a hard time keeping his eyes off Miss Fields, even though her smock was now decorously closed. When he saw the pictures on the daybed, his eyes bugged out of his head.

"The trouble with young cops is they can't keep their minds on murder," Romano commented.

Bart showed Romano the hole in the wall. He took the misshapen pellet from his pocket and handed it to the lieutenant. "I'm no firearms expert," he said, "but I was a Marine, and I'd guess that was a forty-five slug. If it is, and if ballistics shows it was fired from the gun that killed Daphne Temple, you should have no reason to hold James Lennox any longer."

Romano said, "It's a good find, but it's not that easy. It will help Lennox's case, there's no doubt about that, but it won't necessarily mean the D.A.'s going to release him right away. The women only heard one shot fired, but you'd be surprised how many witnesses think shots that come right together are just one shot. Also, you made a mistake in not waiting for me to take the slug out. That would have made it official."

"I didn't know for sure the slug was in the hole," Bart protested. "Miss Fields here saw me take it out. She'll testify to that. You think I planted it? How would I get a slug fired from that particular gun?"

"I wouldn't know, and neither would the D.A.," Romano said patiently. "But it's too bad you didn't wait. It would have been nice and official then."

"You know it wasn't a plant. Why can't you just let it seem you took it out?" Bart asked.

"Because I'm a cop and I do it by the book," Romano answered. "It's the only way I know how to do it. If this came from the murder gun, you've helped Lennox, helped him a lot. But I don't want to get your hopes too high. The D.A. isn't going to let that old man loose until he gets a better story from him or until somebody puts the collar on the murderer."

"But the old man may die down there in that hot little room with this weight on his mind!" Bart flared.

"Listen," said Romano. "You're mad at me. I feel sorry for the old man and I'd like to help him. I'm doing all I can. When you come to your senses you'll see that. But I can't guarantee the D.A. will release old Lennox, no matter what ballistics shows about this slug. It's going to take more than this."

Bart nodded to the girl and started toward the door. He said, "Thanks for your hospitality."

The girl said, "Please! Aren't you going to take a picture?"

"Those pix are just a little too much, even for the *Broadway*

Times," Bart told her. "We've got an owner who is a nice old man, but he draws the line at times. You send me a picture with just a few clothes on, and I'll guarantee to run it."

Chloe said, "My God! You're a funny fellow! You mean you like girls with their *clothes* on?"

nine

Romano and Grierson followed Hardin to the street. Romano said, "We'll have to trouble that young lady again, I'm afraid. I'll have to send police photographers to take a close-up picture of that hole in the wall outside her window. Or maybe they could snap it from the fire escape outside the murder room."

"She shouldn't mind photographers," Grierson said. "Judging from those pictures she's got, she's seen plenty of 'em." He chuckled. "And photographers have seen plenty of her, too," he added.

Bart was standing in front of the darkened premises of the costumer's shop, searching the street for a cab. He turned suddenly to Romano. "I talked to Marty Land," he said. "Doc Raines told Marty that the old man isn't going to live very long if this murder charge keeps hanging over his head. He says medicine isn't going to help, because the trouble's largely psychological. The only thing that's going to save his life is. to clear his name and get him out of that sweatbox down at City right away. Right away. Clearing him next week or next month won't help. He'll probably be dead before then, because this thing has hit him so hard he's lost the will to live. If that slug came from the gun that killed her, it proves that Lennox isn't guilty. She was sitting with her side to the window. The shot that killed her was fired directly into her body from the front, close up. Do you think old Lennox would have shot a bullet out the window, then turned and fired one into her body? You think he was just spraying lead like one of those berserk bad men in a Grade B Western? The women heard one shot. Maybe one person might have been mistaken about that. It's not reasonable to believe two of them could be. You think old Jim was in there fanning a hair trigger?"

Romano shook his head and sighed hopelessly. "I can't make you understand," he said. "There are a lot of things that have to be explained. The point is that the D.A. won't let loose of Lennox until they are explained. The law has taken

65

cognizance of his age and physical condition by putting him in a hospital instead of a jail, and that's as far as the law is going to go right now to give him a break. I'll put the lab to work right away on this slug. If the lands and grooves of the rifling match the gun that killed Daphne Temple, it's a big point in Lennox's favor, but I can't go further in committing myself. I know damn well they'll hold him until there's a bigger break than this."

"That's what the law calls cruel and unusual punishment," Bart said angrily. "You're killing an innocent old man because of puny circumstantial evidence that would never stand up in a court of law."

"Only a person prejudiced in favor of the accused would call it puny," Romano answered. "It's pretty overwhelming in a legal sense. He was on the scene with the gun at his feet and he told a lie. He said his door was locked. A witness who is his friend says the door wasn't locked and wasn't even stuck."

Bart realized it was no use. He saw a cab approaching, its lighted dome signaling that it was vacant. He started to hail it, then changed his mind. He said to Romano, "There are a couple of other things. One, what about Adrian Temple? Are they committing him to an asylum?"

Romano said, "No. The bug doctors say they've hit his knees with the little hammers and had him play with blocks and asked him all the questions bug doctors are supposed to ask. They say he's alcoholic and neurotic, and has a morbid fear of pain, but that he's not insane enough to be committed. Maybe they'd commit him if the family or the police requested it. He hasn't any family now his wife is dead, and the police have no reason to want him committed."

"Coming down and confessing to murders all the time isn't a good reason?" Bart asked.

"We get used to that," Romano replied. "There's hardly ever a killing in this town that half a dozen harmless nuts don't wander in and make a full confession. We've even got special confession cops to handle 'em."

"How long will they hold Temple in the ward at City?"

"They'll probably let him out tomorrow night. With all the crowding they try to keep 'em there only a couple of days for observation. And Temple's wife is being buried day after tomorrow. They might as well let him out in time for the funeral."

"I want to visit Jim Lennox tomorrow morning before I

go to work if he's still alive by then," Bart said. "I guess Marty Land can get me in. He's the old man's lawyer."

"Marty Land can't get you in," Romano said. "He can't get anybody in except himself. You've got to remember that Lennox isn't just a hospital patient. He's a prisoner being held on suspicion of murder. I can get you in. Drop by Manhattan West before you go to the hospital. If I can't go with you, I'll write a note on official stationery. You want to ride downtown? We've got a car here."

Bart realized he was acting like a petulant child, but he refused the offer curtly. Romano and Grierson drove off. After a moment, Hardin found a cab. He directed the driver to the flea circus. He thought a visitor might call at his apartment before the night was done.

No visitor was waiting for him at his apartment. He switched on a light and a floor fan and stripped himself to the waist. He picked up the phone and dialed the number of the women's hotel where Alma Turner resided.

"She fell for it hook, line and sinker, Mr. Hardin," the fortuneteller said. "It was almost frightening. She seemed desperately concerned when I told her about the relationship between you and this mysterious man with the battered face, and she left as if she were shot from a cannon."

Hardin said, "We'll see what happens." He hung up the phone and sat down beside a window that glowed red from the neon sign of Bromberg's Flea Circus and Fun Arcade and poured Irish whisky into a glass, not bothering with ice cubes. He sat in the big, silent room for a long while, whisky sweating from the pores of his naked torso, listening to the eternal hum and screech of Broadway's obbligato. It was nearing midnight when his phone rang.

It was not the voice of the caller he expected. It was Romano. The lieutenant said, "I thought you'd like to know. The slug you pried out of that wall was fired from the gun that killed Daphne Temple."

Bart said, "Thanks. And it does the old man no good at all."

He hung up and poured himself another drink. The glass was barely to his lips when the phone rang again.

A hysterical feminine voice said, "Mr. Hardin? Oh, thank God I caught you. Mr. Hardin, this is Elsa Travers. I've got to see you. I've got to see you right away. I'm desperate, Mr. Hardin. There's a crazy man after me. I'm afraid he's going to kill me."

"Why call me? It sounds like a job for the police."

"I don't know what to do, Mr. Hardin. This concerns you. It concerns the murder, too. But I can't tell you over the phone. Can't you come up here? Please!"

Bart said, "You want me to come to Mrs. Mattingly's?"

Elsa hesitated. "Well, maybe it would be better not to come inside. There are some nosy people here and they stay up late. You know that costumer's shop in the basement? It's fairly dark in the areaway in front of it. Suppose you wait there for me, right in front of the shop door. No one in the house will see you then. How long will it take you to get here?"

"About fifteen minutes," Bart answered.

"I'll come there in just fifteen minutes, then. Please get right up here, Mr. Hardin. I've got to see you."

Bart hung up and put on his shirt and tie. He carried the poplin jacket on his arm. He found a cab outside the building and directed the driver to the corner of Fifty-third and Sixth. He turned the corner on foot. He observed the rooming house from across the street. No one was looking out the windows. He crossed the street hurriedly and descended the two steps to the shop front. He was a few minutes early. He stood looking up at the stoop, waiting for Elsa to come out the door. A dark car was approaching very slowly. It parked in the shadows across the street, the motor running. The door to the rooming house opened and spilled light on Hardin. The car screeched across the street and a volcano seemed to erupt and spray lava pebbles as bullets whined by Hardin's head.

Hardin had been a kid Marine in the Pacific Islands and a captain of Marines in Korea. His response was instinctive, virtually a reflex. He fell prone on his belly. He heard a splintering sound as lead pellets thudded into the suit of armor in the shop window. Deadly little raindrops pinged and skipped on the cement about Hardin's head.

It was over in seconds. The car's motor roared and its wheels screeched away. Hardin lay still for a moment. Then he raised his head. The door of the house above, which had slammed shut when the shooting started, had opened again and Elsa Travers was hurrying down the stoop. Through the shattered shop window Hardin could see a huge carnival mask with one red glass eye. The other eye had been shot out. The single ruby eye stared balefully at Hardin.

As Elsa approached the areaway, Hardin scrambled to his feet. He jumped up the two steps, grabbed the girl's arm. Elsa stifled a scream. Bart shoved her roughly into the foyer of the apartment house next door, where Chloe Fields lived. He rang Chloe's bell. When the buzzer sounded, he kicked the door open and pushed Elsa into the lobby. The self-service elevator was standing at the first floor. Bart pulled Elsa inside it, pressed the top button and kept his finger on it to make sure the elevator's progress would not be interrupted.

He said to Elsa, "There are eight floors in this building and these things don't move fast. It will take a little while to reach the top and get down again. Why did you try to have me killed?"

"But he wasn't trying to kill you! He'd been following me. He thinks he's in love with me and he's a violent, crazy man. I guess he thought I was meeting you. Maybe he would have killed us both."

"Who?"

"A man named Martin. He was a prizefighter once. He was floor manager at a club where I worked and he fell in love with me. He's insane. He's been threatening me and tonight he's been following me. That's why I called you. He must have been parked outside the house."

The elevator was climbing steadily upward. Bart said, "This is too involved to talk about now. Mrs. Mattingly and her roomers are probably out in the street, looking at the damage to the shop. They'll be calling cops. Maybe they'll go back inside before the cops get here and we can slip out and go to my place. We've got a lot to talk about. Your friend Martin wasn't shooting at you. He was shooting at me. And his car wasn't parked out front. It came up just after I arrived. I don't want to see any more cops tonight. I'm sick of cops."

The girl started to say something. Hardin silenced her. The elevator had reached the top floor. As it shuddered to a stop, Hardin pushed the lowest button and reversed its progress.

There was someone waiting for them in the lobby.

It was Chloe Fields. She still wore the smock. It was demurely buttoned now, but her dimpled bare knees showed beneath it.

She said to Bart, "Hey, it's you! Did you ring my bell? It rang a few minutes ago and nobody came up. Hey, what's going on? There were a lot of fireworks under the front window, then you rang my bell and now you come sneaking off the elevator with another girl. And you've got dirt all over you. What's this all about?"

She was staring at Elsa. "Say, I know you!" she declared. "You had a specialty spot at the Seventh Veil when I was in the line. You used a live dove in your number."

My God, Bart thought, more feathers.

Hardin said to Chloe, "You want to get your picture in the paper, don't you, sugar?"

"Sure, I do."

"Then just keep your pretty little mouth shut about this."

Chloe clapped her small hands. "Blackmail!" she said. "I always did want to blackmail somebody. When you going to run it, mister?"

"As soon as you get me one with just a few more clothes on," Bart said. "Not too many clothes, though. There's no reason to overdo it."

Chloe pouted. "It takes a lot of money to pay these theatrical photographers. Why can't you use the ones I've got?"

Bart fished in his pocket, handed her a fifty-dollar bill. "Hire yourself a good photographer," he said. "And drop the print off when it's finished."

"Gee!" cried the girl. "I'm a real blackmailer! Little Chloe is finally getting smart."

"Start earning your money," Bart said. "Take a look outside and tell us if anyone's in front of the house next door."

Chloe went out into the foyer, returned in a moment and said, "There's a funny little fat man with the damnedest mustache and goatee I ever saw. He's staring at that one-eyed mask in the busted shop window."

"Go back and signal us when he leaves."

Chloe beckoned to them presently. Bart took Elsa Travers' arm and hurried her out to the street. He headed for Sixth Avenue, in the opposite direction from the rooming house. He heard a police siren just as he reached Sixth Avenue and hailed a cab. They're a little late, he thought.

Elsa did not speak as the cab rolled toward Bart's flat. Her gaunt, pallid face was set in rigid lines and her dark eyes stared straight ahead. For the first time Bart became conscious of her costume. She wore black velvet matador slacks that reached just below her knees and a knit silk turtle-neck sweater with long sleeves. The clothes were molded to her sinuous body. Add some plumes and she might resemble the little magician's feathered serpent, he thought.

When they were inside his apartment, Bart said, "Sit down. Do you want a drink? I'm going to have one. It upsets me to get shot at."

Elsa nodded dumbly.

Bart poured the drinks.

He sipped his, stood over Elsa, staring down at her.

"All right," said Bart. "You set me up for a clay pigeon. We won't bother about that, because your boy friend missed. But there's an old man lying in a locked room. He's accused of murder and he may be dying. I'm going to get him out of there. I'll do anything I have to do to get him out. Start talking. And talk straight."

Elsa said, "Last winter I was working at a club called the Seventh Veil. There's a floor manager there. That's a polite term for a bouncer. He was a brute and I was deadly afraid of him. His name was Stony Martin. He'd been a prizefighter, I think."

Elsa gulped her drink.

Bart said, "Keep talking."

"He made passes at me. It was horrible. I'm a very sensitive person. I'm really psychic, of course. Everyone who knows me well realizes that. I could sense the aura of this man. It was bad, evil. There was violence in him, and death. But he kept forcing his attentions on me. He nearly drove me insane. He said he was in love with me. He asked me to live with him and he even offered to marry me. He pursued me everywhere I went and made my life a hell. He was revolting, but I was afraid of him. I tried not to show my loathing because I knew he could do me harm."

She finished her drink, held out her glass to Bart. She said, "I don't drink much, but all this horror is too much for me."

Bart poured her drink, said, "Keep talking."

"One day this Martin gave me a gun. He virtually forced me to take it. He said I needed it for my protection. I was living alone then, in a cheap hotel, and there were some very disagreeable men in the place. They said the most offensive things to me when I passed them in the halls, and they knocked on my door late at night. But I took the gun only because I was afraid to refuse it. I did not want this Martin to fly into one of his tempers. They were terrible. I think Martin sold guns, stolen guns. It was one of his rackets."

"What kind of gun did he give you?" Bart asked.

"I don't know. I know nothing about such things. It's

rather small, with a pearl handle. I've got it in my purse. I've been carrying it today, ever since he threatened me. I was going to throw it away. It's in my bag."

She had been wearing a large leather shoulder bag. She had laid it on a table. She rose now and went toward it.

Bart bolted in front of her, grabbed the bag and found the gun. "That would have been too easy, sweetheart," he said.

The gun was a small Continental model not often seen in this country. It was a twenty-five-caliber Waldman Automatic. The gun that had fired the shot which killed Daphne Temple and the slug Bart had dug from the wall was a Colt forty-five.

Bart said, "Sit down." He put her bag back on the table, pocketed the pistol. "I'll keep the gun," he said. "I think I'd feel safer. I don't like getting shot at more than once a night."

"You're being ridiculous, Hardin," Elsa Travers said. "You know that, don't you? I'm deadly afraid of guns. I wouldn't know how to use one. And certainly I have no reason to want to shoot you."

"You set me up pretty nicely for your boy friend Martin," Bart said. "But we won't go into that. Tell me about Martin's threat today."

"He called me tonight about eight o'clock. He said something dreadful was going to happen if I didn't meet him. He said he would see I was arrested for the murder of Daphne Temple."

She finished her second whisky. "I finally agreed, because I was afraid not to. He's psychotic. He'll do anything. I met him in a bar near the Seventh Veil where he works. He told me that if I didn't give myself to him, come and live with him, he would go to the police and tell them he had sold me the gun that killed poor Daphne. I knew he would, even if it meant prison for him. He's quite mad. And I was afraid. People know that I'm in love with Adrian Temple. When you're in love as I am you radiate an aura that even insensitive people can feel. They know. Everyone knew I was in love with Adrian. It's quite hopeless. He's never loved anyone but Daphne, but it would be a motive for my killing his wife."

"You knew the gun that Martin gave you wasn't the one that killed Daphne," Bart said. "Why were you afraid?"

"He would have lied. He would have said he gave me the other gun, the one that was used for murder. There's nothing a man like that won't do if the compulsion is strong enough."

"So you thought you'd solve everything by having him kill me? I don't quite follow that."

"That's absurd. I can't stand the thought of violence. I called you because I thought you might help me. You're strong. I can feel your aura, Hardin. It's strong and dependable. I needed someone like that. I knew Martin had followed me home, but I though he'd left before I called you. He must have come back in the car. He's insanely jealous. When he saw us together he must have tried to murder us. Oh, I'm afraid!"

"We weren't together," Hardin told her.

"He must have seen we had a rendezvous." She rose and walked toward Hardin. She clutched his arm, the long red nails biting into his flesh. Her body flattened against him and moved sinuously.

"Oh please," she said, her voice husky now. "Oh, please, Hardin! I need you. Help me, Hardin."

Her eyes were closed and he felt her breath on his face. Hardin stood still as she continued to move against him and murmur, "Please!"

Then he shoved her roughly away from him. "Get out of here," he said. "I've got things to do. Besides, you shouldn't depend on me. I'm going to send you up for murder if I can."

ten

They had given the tiny old man in the loose hospital gown
a sedative early in the evening, when they turned the lights
out in the little sweat-box of a room he occupied, but it was
after midnight now and he was tossing restlessly on the damp
bed. In hospitals they do it by the book, and the book says
that heart cases should not lie flat, so they had left the bed
tilted. The old man lay in a half-sitting posture and this added
to his discomfort. The room was dimly lighted by the reflec-
tion from the kitchens directly beneath him and the bulbs
in the corridor across the narrow areaway.

Outside the locked door of the room a fat, grizzled cop
sat uncomfortably on a hard straight chair. He had almost
reached retirement age and he had never gained a better
rank than patrolman. A copy of a morning tabloid and a pair
of glasses were on his lap. He had tried to read the sports
pages because he was a Dodger fan, but the perspiration made
his glasses mist over and the corridor light was very dim. He
sat there now, perspiring and cursing his luck and scratching
surreptitiously at his fat thighs, which were covered with a
heat rash. He had thought this would be a cushy assignment
in the heat wave. The heat had made his feet swell and he
dreaded any job that meant much walking. But even his railroad flat in Brooklyn was far cooler than this. He had never
dreamed that hospitals could be so hot. He had imagined
they were air-cooled in the summer. He wondered vaguely if
the private rooms outside the locked wards had air conditioning.

The old cop didn't think of Lennox as a murder suspect
or even as a sick man. He merely thought of him as one of
the thousands and thousands of citizens whose unpredictable
conduct had made his life miserable for thirty years. Citizens were always doing the wrong thing at the wrong time.
They couldn't commit their damned crimes when you were
beginnng your tour of duty. They had to hold up somebody
just about the time that you were going home to a midnight

74

snack and a bottle of Bud, and they had to hold 'em up right
in front of your eyes so you couldn't avoid taking them in,
and that meant you had to hang around the precinct for
hours when you were supposed to be off duty and you never
got a dime of extra pay for it. Take this old man. He couldn't
wait for cool weather to knock off some young chick. He had
to time it so that a cop would have to sit outside his door
in the hottest place in New York on the hottest night of
the whole damned year. Citizens had no consideration for the
police who protected them.

Jesus, why couldn't they invent a really cool uniform for
summer, he wondered. He'd taken a chance and loosened his
tie and unbuttoned his collar, but he couldn't risk more than
that. The locked wards were full of inconsiderate citizens
who kept on committing crimes even in weather like this,
and the brass might walk by any moment to interview one of
them. He'd heard that down in Miami or the West Indies
or somewhere cops wore open-throated, short-sleeved shirts
and those funny pants called walking shorts,

He glanced at his watch and saw that time was crawling
by. He had many hours still to go.

The heavy metal doors of the big locked ward were clanging open. An intern came out, accompanied by a heavy-
bosomed, motherly-looking Negro nurse. The intern locked
the prison-like door. The nurse was starchy and unwilted
in the heat. She radiated a kind of inner contentment that
defied small discomforts and inconveniences. There's a woman
who likes her job, the policeman thought. There's a woman
who's happy. I know a few cops like that. Just a few.

As the nurse came abreast of the policeman, she said, "My
gracious me, you do look hot, Mr. Policeman! Maybe I
I better get you some salt pills. We're short, but we can
spare a couple for a man who looks as hot as you."

The old cop said, "I'd rather have a big, cold glass of
beer, miss."

The nurse laughed heartily. "Now wouldn't that go good,
though? But we don't keep it in the medicine cabinet. I
guess my boys back there in the big ward would like a glass
of beer, too. A lot of them are alkies. They even beg you for
paraldehyde." She shuddered. "Can't even stand to smell that
stuff, myself. The doctor and I have just been back to one of
them. He's a real weird one, too. Temple, the husband of that
girl that got killed. Don't know why the cops should put

that poor man here, he's got enough grief, goodness knows. He's getting out tomorrow, I understand. He's scared to take his sleeping pill because he thinks we're going to slip up in the night and jab a needle in him or do something that will hurt. Now wouldn't you think a man whose wife's just been murdered would have more than that to worry himself about?"

She inclined her head toward the closed door of the little room. "The one I feel really sorry for, though, is that old man inside, the one they say murdered Temple's wife. They think they do the serious cases a favor when they put 'em in this little room. It gets 'em away from the screamers in the big ward, of course, but it's no favor in this hot weather, believe me. I gave the old man a wash and a pill and I'm telling you even I almost fainted in that room. And I don't usually feel the heat much."

Inside the room, the old man was stupefied by the heat and drugs, but he did not sleep. The clanging of the pots and pans in the kitchen below kept reminding him of something. It seemed to be important, but he couldn't remember what it was. Maybe it was the rattling of armor in the battle scene in *Richard III*, or the clashing of rapiers in *Cyrano de Bergerac*.

Then suddenly he remembered and he jerked himself bolt upright on the bed.

He had heard a metallic clang on that awful night—how long ago now? It couldn't be just yesterday.

He had heard the clang of metal just after he had heard the shot.

He had been asleep, but he was sure. The shot had awakened him, then he had heard the clang of metal, and now that suddenly appeared as all-important. Now he knew what the metallic clang had been.

Had he told the police? Had he told Bart? His memory was all confused.

"Bart!" he called in a feeble voice. "Bart! Bart! Please come here, Bart!"

The door opened and the policeman and the nurse came in. The policeman stood just inside the door. He said, "What's the matter with you, mister?"

The nurse went to the bed and laid a plump hand on the old man's hot and sweaty forehead. "You want something, honey?" she asked as if she were speaking to a child.

"I've got to see Bart," Lennox said. "Bart Hardin. Please send him to me. I have to tell him something."

The nurse's hand smoothed his head. "What you want to tell him, honey?"

The old man stared up at the nurse and his eyes became dead and swimming again.

"I—I've forgotten," he said weakly.

eleven

After Elsa left, Bart walked into the bathroom and looked at himself in the long mirror on the door. Dirt from the areaway where he had fallen to dodge the bullets was caked on his shirt and his poplin pants. There was a jagged tear in the trousers and a scuffed red knee showed through. A piece of flying glass had nicked the lobe of his left ear. He stripped and showered, then went to the wardrobe to find another suit. There was only one summer-weight left. It was a blue linen job. He should have remembered to take the others to the cleaners, he thought. He put on a clean shirt, finished dressing and went into the living room. He poured himself half a tumbler of Irish. It was one-thirty in the morning but there was no hurry. The place where he was going stayed open until four, and the men he wanted to see would be busiest when the drunks got really boisterous. He was fairly sure to find the man on duty.

He needed a little fortification for what he planned to do. He supposed it was a senseless thing, that it was giving in to the compulsion of personal anger. But perhaps it would serve as a warning, scare them off from making another attempt on his life. He didn't want to get shot before he had old Jim Lennox out of that hospital room.

He finished his whisky and left the building. He walked uptown through the heat haze that was further fueled by the billion blinking bulbs of Broadway's signs. He walked north and then he turned east.

The Seventh Veil was on a street known as Sucker Alley and the Nudist Colony because it was the location of a dozen or more traps where female performers were stripped and male customers were fleeced. Carnival barkers with faces that belonged on "wanted" posters stood in front of each of the dives, and at this hour of a hot summer night they virtually tried to drag passersby inside, for the heat wave had stifled Broadway's flesh business.

The barker in front of the Seventh Veil was chanting, "The air is cool and the girls are hot. Show going on right now. Plenty of ringside tables. Get a close-up view of the girls, men."

The Seventh Veil was one of the worst of the traps. It had a reputation for padded checks, free-for-all fights and general unpleasantness that made all but the most unwary customers, such as soldiers and sailors, steer clear of it. It couldn't possibly have existed on the income of its cabaret business. Like many of the other Syndicate clubs, it served other purposes. New acts were tried out here, and tired old acts were hired for a pittance. It was also a drop for the numbers racket, a steer joint for call girls and, lately, a clearing house for hot guns.

When Bart turned into the place, the doorman was so overjoyed that he almost fell down opening the red-painted, chromium-trimmed door.

All the night clubs of the Nudist Colony have dusky interiors and they smell of whisky, cigarette smoke and strong perfume. The Seventh Veil was no exception.

As Bart entered, a hatcheck girl with a hard face and incredibly conical breasts said, "Jesus God, another one without a hat. In summer we should make 'em check their shoes, like the Japanese. But I guess they'd all go barefoot then."

Benny Speakman, who fronted for the Syndicate as owner of the sucker trap, was standing in the small lobby near the hatcheck pitch. He was a middle-aged man with heavy shoulders and a broad, flat-featured face, and he was blue-jowled even when he was freshly shaved. He had once been a fight manager on Jacobs Beach. When he recognized Bart, he said unpleasantly, "Well, well, another free-loader. Don't tell me the joint is finally going to get a break in the *Broadway Times*."

Bart said, "No free-load, Benny. I wouldn't free-load at a trap where the whisky's watered."

Benny said, "Tonight I can't even give whisky away. If you're looking for a call girl, all of them I know are out of town. They can't take the heat. Or maybe you just dropped around because you like to see my pretty face."

"I want to see a mug who works for-you. Stony Martin," Bart replied.

"That crumb-bum!" Benny flared. "He's supposed to be the floor man. He's had lots of visitors tonight. A while back a dame who used to dance here with a goddamn mangy dove dropped around to see him and he went out with her. Just walked right out without saying a damn word to anybody. He's got a thing for this dove dancer, Elsa, whatever the hell her name is. He used to run after her with his tongue hanging out when she and her goddamn mangy dove were lousing up the joint. I'll never forgot that dove. It thought everything in the trap was a bathroom. Once it was molting and it flew out into the kitchen and sprayed tailfeathers in the chicken à la king. I threw her and her dove out on their keisters. But that Stony, he had a thing for her and she could wrap him around her little finger. He still must have the thing, I guess. She comes around to see him tonight, but thank God she don't bring the lousy dove with her. Stony goes out, and fifteen minutes later two big Marines start breaking the joint apart just because they got a fifteen-dollar check for some beer and chicken sandwiches. They think we operate for charity? They think we're the U.S.O. or something, maybe?

"Maybe Marines just like to break things," Hardin said.

"These did. Me and the waiters had to do the bounce and I skinned two knuckles. I don't know how that dame can lead Stony around by the nose like she does. She don't appeal to me, her or her goddamn dove, if she's still got it. She's one of them dames with bones. Dames with bones don't send me. Never have. What the hell do you want to see Stony about?"

"I've got a little business with him."

"Business? I never thought you'd need hardware. You ain't gonna take him out of here again, are you? There's a couple of soused-up saps from Syracuse are gonna get a real big check when the floor grind's over. They ain't as tough as the Marines, but I might need Stony."

"I just want to talk to Stony privately," Bart told Benny.

"I let him use the little office in back for his hardware business," Benny said. "It counts as part of his pay. But don't use big words when you talk to him. Stony caught too many on the button. When they forget to duck, their brains turn into scrambled eggs."

Benny inclined his head, signaling Bart to follow him. He led Hardin through the club, up an almost impassably narrow aisle between the wall and the clustered tables. Few of the tables were occupied. The floor show was on and a blonde with bosoms was wriggling her body directly in front of a table where three drunken and middle-aged playboys sat ogling her. The blonde held the brassière she had just removed in her hand and she sang "Moonlight and Roses" in a tinny voice that the brasses of the band couldn't drown out.

Benny took Bart back of the orchestra stand and opened the door to his small office. He motioned Bart inside and left. The walls were covered with pictures of girls who were almost completely nude. Bart thought of little Chloe and her publicity photographs as he waited for Stony Martin to appear.

Martin came into the room. He was a big man. He had fought as a light heavy, but he would never make the weight now. Gloved fists had battered his face into a vacuous caricature. Like many old fighters, he resembled a very ugly baby.

Stony said, "You want me?"

Bart said, "My name's Bart Hardin."

He waited for a reaction, but Stony's flattened face was eminently adapted to masking emotion.

"So?" said Stony.

"I used to see you fight at St. Nick's and the Garden."

"So?"

"I saw Fighting Phil Casazza flatten you with a left jab to the shoulder when he was coming up."

"Smart guy," said Stony.

"I saw Bicycle Blake take you at the Garden with a left hook that couldn't squash a grape."

"You're a real smart guy. I like smart guys. I get kicks from belting them," said Stony.

"You're no better with a gun than you were with your fists," Bart said pleasantly. "I feel just fine and you wasted all those bullets."

Stony averted his eyes momentarily. Then he said, "You talk real crazy, mister. A wheel, that's what you are. A real gone hipster. Go on. Have fun."

Stony Martin's hand was in his pocket. He did not pull a gun. He took a pair of black leather gloves from the pocket. The gloves had heavy cross-stitching over the knuckles. The stitching could cut and tear a man's face, Hardin thought.

Hardin said, "Why are you putting your gloves on, Stony? Are you getting cold?"

"I'm going to belt you, mister," Stony answered. "I'm going to belt you and I don't want to bruise my knuckles."

"Like this?" asked Bart. His left whipped up from the hip to Stony's chin and the right crossed flush into the middle of Stony's battered, expressionless face.

Stony sat down on the floor.

Stony opened his mouth and sucked in air. He shook his head to clear it. His gloved hand stole toward the blackjack in his pocket. He braced himself to spring.

Hardin kicked him in the face. Stony's head bounced off the wall and made a loud sound.

Hardin said, "Stay on the floor, Stony. You'll feel more at home. I'll even count ten if you want me to."

Blood was coming out of Stony's mouth. He moved the mouth and said, "I'm going to kill you, mister."

"The trouble is, you have to get up off the floor first," Hardin answered as he kicked him in the face again.

The sound was louder as Stony's head hit the wall this time. Stony closed his eyes.

The office door flew open. Benny Speakman looked down at Stony.

He shook his head at Hardin. "You shouldn't come around here messing up the help like that," he said. "It ain't good manners."

"Your boy threw bullets at me when he was out tonight," Hardin said. "A whole gunful of bullets. I didn't like it much."

Benny's eyes were hard. He said, "If he did, it wasn't business. I know nothing about it. I don't know what he might think up with those scrambled eggs inside his head. But don't louse up my trap, Hardin. That's a warning. You're fooling with tough people now. This ain't no Golden Gloves. You stay out of here from now on. A long way out. I don't want what's gonna happen to happen in my trap. Stony ain't got much mind left, but what he's got remembers. He's a hardware dealer, Hardin. He ain't just a punk taking dives when we tell him any more. When they close their fists on metal, they get cocky. It ain't business and I ain't responsible. Remember that."

Hardin said, "It's business, and you're responsible. Moe Selig and the Syndicate aren't going to like it if they lose a drop like this because you let the hired help get out of line. I could run a story in the *Broadway Times* about the numbers and the fifty-dollar girls and the hardware business, with a name and address in it. If that happened, there'd be a big, fat padlock on your door and a little printed notice that the police had closed the premises. Maybe you'd better talk to Stony, Benny. If you don't, some of the boys might be around to talk to you."

Hardin stepped out of the office. He turned to Benny, said, "I'm going to get a drink at the bar, Benny. I'm going to pay for it. Tell the bartender to pour it from the boss's bottle, will you?"

twelve

Hardin finished his drink at the bar, paid for it, tipped the bartender. In the small lobby of the night club he entered a phone booth and called Marty Land's private number, despite the fact that it was now two o'clock in the morning. Marty answered the phone himself.

Hardin said, "I know it's an ungodly hour, but I want to come up and talk to you. Things have been happening. You hadn't gone to bed, had you?"

"I was reading," Marty answered. "Between this society playboy I'm defending against a procuring charge and poor old Lennox and the heat, I'm getting bugged. Whenever I get bugged, I sit down and read a certain book. It calms me down. Come on up. I've got some Irish."

"It'll take a little while," Hardin told him. "I'm going to walk. When you're bugged, you read. When I'm bugged, I walk."

Hardin hung up. He started out the door of the club, then he turned back and tossed a dollar to the hard-faced hatcheck girl. "That's a deposit against next winter," he said.

He walked east and turned uptown on Madison.

The neighborhood was desolate at this time of the morning. It was the center of the advertising and television industries and there were many bars and restaurants, but most of them closed early because the majority of their weekday customers commuted to Long Island and Westchester and Connecticut and ran their lives on railroad timetables.

Marty had apparently sent his man to bed. He opened the door for Hardin himself and led him in to the gracious living room with its pastoral Blakelocks and Inneses. A high-fidelity phonograph was playing MacDowell's "Woodland Sketches." He had a bottle of Irish ready and poured Bart a drink. He took cognac himself. He picked up a book that was lying open beside a high-backed wing chair.

"This is what I read when the snakes are out," he said. "It always calms me. *Walden*, by Thoreau. Have you ever read it?"

Bart said, "I always thought *Walden* was a book like *War and Peace*. Everybody pretends he's read it, but nobody really has."

Marty said, "I've read it. Not once, but many times. It's a browsing kind of book and it makes you feel peaceful. In a a way I suppose reading *Walden* is a nostalgic journey into the past for me. I'm a Proper Bostonian by birth, did you know that? Thoreau and Emerson were required reading for all Proper Bostonians. My father gave me this book on my fifteenth birthday."

"I always thought you must have grown up on Broadway, just like I did," Bart said. "My dad rented that apartment above the flea circus when I was a baby, after my mother died. I've never lived anywhere else, except for a couple of hitches in the Marines."

"I grew up in Louisburg Square," Marty replied. "You ever hear of it? It's the very proper heart of very proper Boston. On Beacon Hill. A little square of old, old houses with a park in the middle. There's an iron gate to the park and only the people in the old houses have a key to it. I was born in one of those old houses. They've got windowpanes of crinkled, lavender glass so the vulgar people on the outside can't even look in on them. It's going now, but up to a few years ago, Louisburg Square was the last refuge of the dying race of Brahmins. For generations they sat in the lavender twilight and drank India tea from Wedgwood cups at four o'clock exactly and discussed Thoreau and Emerson and Harvard and the spring cotillion. There was a noisy, evil world somewhere, but it never touched them. They had the lavender panes in their windows and the iron fence around their park to keep the world out. The head of the family went to business, of course, very respectable business, but he never brought the outside world back home with him. Louisburg Square was an island and it was sacrosanct. So I grew up there, and now I'm Moe Selig's attorney and they call me the Broadway Mouth."

"How'd you ever get to the Big Street with a background like that?" Bart asked.

"I could make a lot of explanations. I might say I was one of Scott Fitzgerald's sad young men, that I was in revolt. Actually, I suppose, I just wanted the big money and the things the big money could buy. And if you want to hand yourself a boffo, take a look at what the money's bought me. It's all around you here, a house pretty much like the one I left in Louisburg Square, shuttered and air-conditioned against the sounds and smells of the noisy, violent world that supports me. It's my island. It cost me a hell of a lot more than the twenty-eight dollars, twelve and a half cents that Thoreau paid for his house at Walden."

Marty sipped his brandy. "Even my father would have approved of this house," he said. "But he would hardly approve of me. I followed all my ancestors to Groton and Harvard and then I lit out on my own. I hit the Big Street. My father was a lawyer, too. He thought corporation law was the only sort that a respectable man could practice. I could have gone into his firm. Instead I've got Moe Selig and the Broadway Times for clients. My old man wouldn't have invited a criminal lawyer into his house any more than he would have invited the garbage collector. Oh, well, I wanted money and I've made it and I've had my kicks and boffos. But sometimes I get nostalgic. I read Thoreau and I think I'll retire and find a place in the country. I'm not quite fifty and I've got all the dough a single man could ever use, even if he had a weakness for filling inside straights. The only trouble is, I can't find any country that has moons as golden as Blakelock's or trees as dark and clumpy as the ones that Innes painted."

Marty splashed more Irish into Hardin's glass. "You didn't come here at this hour of the morning to talk about people who live in lavender-glass houses and drink tea from Wedgwood cups," he said. "What's on your mind? Oh, first. You're suspicious of this girl, Elsa. I can tell that. I've done a little private detecting to earn the fee that Seling doesn't know he's paying me for defending Lennox. I've found out a couple of things. She was in love with Temple, all right. Everybody seems to agree on that. And there was some insurance. Adrian and Daphne had insured each other's lives for twenty-five thousand when they were a dance team. That was sound business. Somehow Adrian managed to keep up the insurance payments after Daphne was hurt and the team broke up and he hit the skids. Twenty-five grand would look like a lot of money to Elsa, who spent most of her time in strip-house grinds before she met Adrian. If she thinks he'll marry her, the money might be an added motive for her killing Daphne."

Bart told Land the story Selig had related about Elsa obtaining a forty-five-caliber army gun from Stony Martin. He then told him of Elsa's producing the twenty-five-caliber Waldman and her claim that it was the gun Martin had given her.

Marty chuckled. "That Selig," he said. "He's like the oriental monkeys in reverse. He sees all evil and hears all evil and in this case he's even speaking a little evil, considering how close-mouthed he and his kind usually are. In a way, knowing a character like that has been almost worth selling my birthright for a mess of Selig. It's not only that he and the others have a right to their day in court with a competent attorney to represent them. It's not even the money I take from him. It's studying him as an important figure of our times and particularly of the Street. In some ways, Selig and I are a lot alike. I've cut corners and maybe dirtied my hands a little to get a lot of money, and now I'm going soft and sentimental about my respectable background. Selig's done everything including murder, and yet I honestly think the thing he wants most, now that he's growing old, is respectability. He's proud as hell of the fact that he's associated with men like Maddox Slade in theatrical ventures and that he can afford a lawyer who lives in a house like this. It's hard for legitimate businessmen to refuse mob money. It's about the only big chunk of liquid money that's left in these days of exorbitant taxes. I'd say about a quarter of Selig's enterprises are entirely legitimate. He owns a couple of Broadway theatres outright and he's landlord of a big apartment house on Park Avenue. He also operates a super market in the Bronx. His daughter goes to one of the most fashionable women's colleges in the East, only she doesn't go there under the name of Selig. That's Selig's cross. When he's respectable, he has to be anonymous."

Bart said, "One of the less respectable mobsters took a shot at me tonight. Several shots, in fact."

He told Land of what had happened in front of the costumer's shop. He told him of what he had done to Stony

Marty said, "Maybe you did the best thing in clobbering him. Sometimes I think the direct action that you guys who have been conditioned in a couple of wars take is the only answer to the hoods. The mobs have got rich because our legal system and our social customs aren't geared to answering force with the only weapon it understands. If that boxer with the scrambled brains is really gone for the girl Elsa and she thinks you know too much, she might persuade him to take another shot at you and this time he might not miss. The only stronger force working on his addled mind is the mob itself. His employer, Benny Speakman, is in the mob and if he's afraid Stony's quarrel with you may affect his business, he'll put the arm on his hired boy real quick."

Hardin said, "A ventriloquist's dummy named Woodenhead Willie got himself into the act. He advised me to take a look in the house next door to Mrs. Mattingly's. I took a good, close look at it tonight. There was a slug from a forty-five in the hole. Romano tells me it was fired from the same gun that killed Daphne Temple."

Land nodded gravely. "I know all about it," he said. "Romano called me tonight. He's trying to help us, Hardin, even though you won't believe it. He's concerned for the old man, too. I'm sorry you found that slug."

"Why?"

"Because it hurts our case. According to the evidence, there are just two people who could possibly have killed Daphne Temple at the time the shot was heard. One was Lennox. The other we have to offer is Elsa, and the fact that we know she had that gun, even though neither Selig nor Martin will testify for us, is a strong point. Elsa could have had the gun in her handbag, gone upstairs when she and Mrs. Mattingly came back from the theatre, shot Daphne, screamed as if she'd heard the shot. She could have locked Lennox's door on the way to Daphne's room. She could have thrown the gun out on the fire escape, stood there in the hall, with the door of Daphne's room closed, and waited for Mrs. Mattingly to come upstairs and discover the body with her. But Mrs. Mattingly heard only one shot. That knocks our theory into the well-known hat with the cocked-up brim."

"She could have fired two shots. Mrs. Mattingly could have been mistaken," Bart said.

"Of course," Land admitted. "Witnesses are often mistaken in what they see and hear. A good cross-examiner relies upon that basic fact. Eyewitness evidence is often the most unreliable evidence there is. So is ear-witness evidence. I'd bring that up in a court of law. I'm convinced it would establish reasonable doubt with a jury. But we can't wait to get to a court of law. We've got to get that old man out of that little room. That's the urgent thing. And we've got to get this load off his mind. This reasonable-doubt theory of ours would probably be enough to make a jury acquit Lennox. It isn't enough to make the D.A. release Lennox right now."

"When Elsa threw that gun out on the fire escape, it could have gone off," Bart said. "That would account for the bullet in the wall."

Marty said, "I was 'way ahead of you on that one, cousin. It was the first thing I thought of, and I presented the argument to Romano when he called. There are two big drawbacks. In the first place, both Mrs. Mattingly and Lennox himself heard one shot and one shot only. In the second place, Romano explained that if the gun had been discharged when it hit the fire-escape platform, the bullet would probably have gone through the window of that girl next door, low down. Anyway, the hole in the wall was at least five feet above the level of the platform."

Bart rose and began to stride about the big room.

"You're stall-walking," Land said. "That's bad. Maybe I should lend you my copy of Thoreau. It's better for the nerves than celery tonic."

Hardin said, "I guess it's the old guilt complex. I took this thing in my own hands and went at it my own way. I took the short cuts you mentioned a minute ago, because Romano insisted it had to be done by the book and it's going to take too long to do it by the book. So I dug the shell out of the hole in the wall before I even called the cops, and Romano says that was a mistake. Now you tell me the biggest mistake of all was even finding that hole in the wall to begin with. Instead of helping old Jim, it's hurt his case. I guess, though, that if I hadn't told the cops, that ventriloquist, Montgomery, would have had his dummy inform them. Montgomery seems to get a kick out of having the dummy do most of his talking. Apparently he's been standing there at his window, on the floor above, staring at a kid across the way who doesn't wear too many clothes, and that's how he happened to see the hole."

"You shouldn't blame yourself," the lawyer said. "The cops were sure to see the hole eventually, anyway, and find out what was in it. They just didn't look too hard at first because they figured the other shot from the gun had been fired at some previous date in a different place, in all probability."

"There's one more thing I didn't tell you or anyone else," Bart said. "I didn't tell you because in view of the facts we know and the timing of the thing, it seemed completely unimportant. That Mexican magician with the funny mustache, Sandrean, was seen entering the house a few minutes before ten. No one saw him leave, but he was back in the stage show at the Music Hall at ten-twenty, so he couldn't have stayed long. But of course he might have been there long enough to kill Daphne. He admits he was there, but says he broke his false teeth in his dressing room and returned to get a spare set."

"It doesn't mean too much, I'm afraid," said Marty. "Lennox was in the next room and he didn't hear a shot at that time. He might have been so sound asleep it didn't wake him, but that's unlikely. A shot from a forty-five usually makes a hell of a lot of noise. But what's more important is that Lennox did hear a shot at a few minutes to eleven, and so did Mrs. Mattingly and Elsa. They heard one shot."

"Those damned feathers," Hardin went on. "They're bugging me, too. Why should a murderer spread goose feathers around a corpse? And the feather motif keeps repeating itself. Daphne wore a feathered costume in her Little Goose dance. Sandrean had a feathered serpent as the climax of his act, and he thinks the serpent is symbolic of evil and revenge. Elsa used a feathered dove in her night club specialty number. Mrs. Mattingly had a pillow stuffed with goose feathers stolen from her linen closet, and I happened to notice she wears a feathered negligee around the house. Even the colored maid, Dora, has a feather duster."

Marty chuckled. "It's an old story to me," he said. "When some perfectly ordinary, everyday object takes on importance in a case, you begin to notice it for the first time and you seem to run into it everywhere you go. It's not that there's suddenly a greater quantity of the particular substance than there ever was before. It's just that you're conscious of it. I remember a murder case I defended once a long time ago. A tiny, almost microscopic sliver of colored glass was an important piece of police evidence. You'd be surprised how many things are made of colored glass when you start enumerating them. Drinking tumblers, pitchers, vases, martini mixers, beads, cuff links, trimming on women's dresses, church windows. This particular piece was a chip from a man's artificial eye, it turned out. I found that out and saved a client from the electric chair, but I was seeing objects made of colored glass in my dreams for months afterward."

Bart said, "Marty, are we going to get that old man out of that little room in time?"

Land rose, pushed Hardin into a chair. "Sit down," he said. "Sit down and relax. Marty never gives up just because the snakes are out. The snakes are always out at some point of every murder case I ever handled. When that happens, Marty comes home and reads Thoreau and plays MacDowell's 'Woodland Sketches' on his phonograph and pretty soon he's relaxed and his mind starts working straight again."

Land filled Hardin's glass, handed it to him. "There's one thing, at least," he said. "I talked Maddox Slade out of running a piece in his paper denying that Lennox had any connection with the *Broadway Times.* I think the trout with a white wine sauce and almond dressing was the clincher. Slade fancies himself a gourmet, you know. Anyway, he's a smart man. He has to be smart to have made all that nice money. He's smart enough to realize he needs you and he needs me, even if we both see through his pretentiousness and refuse to yes him."

The telephone at the far end of the big room rang.

Marty said, "My God, I hope nobody's murdered anybody at this time of night."

He walked briskly across the room and picked up the receiver.

He said, "Hello. Oh, Lieutenant Romano! You work late hours."

Then he listened and interjected only a few meaningless comments. "Uh-*huh,*" and, "I *see,*" he said a time or two. Finally he said, "That's very fair of you, Lieutenant. Hardin is up here. May I bring him, too?"

He was apparently answered in the affirmative. He said, "Thank you. Thank you for calling me about this, Lieutenant."

Then he hung up the phone and crossed the room slowly, his eyes on Hardin. He looked down at Bart. His dark, handsome face, marked only faintly by the lines of dissipation, was grave.

He said, "We just lost our only suspect, Hardin."

"What?"

"Elsa Travers. She's just killed herself."

thirteen

There was heavy silence in the big room. The phonograph that had been playing chamber music had shut itself off automatically long before. Only the low hum of the air-conditioners wedged behind the Fortuny prints that draped the windows could be heard now.

Finally Bart said, "Did she leave a note? Did she confess she murdered Daphne? Can we get old Jim out of that little room now, Marty?"

Land shook his head. "If she left a note, they haven't found it," he answered. "Romano has just arrived. She apparently jumped off the roof twenty or thirty minutes ago. Mrs. Mattingly had left the skylight on the top floor open for ventilation. She climbed the little ladder to the skylight, climbed through and jumped to the sidewalk. She landed in the areaway in front of that costumer's shop and she was killed immediately. It will be one of those 'jumped or fell' verdicts, of course. Homicide wouldn't ordinarily be in on it. But because of the address and because she was connected with the Temple murder, Romano went up. He's willing to let us come there if we want to and hear anything there is to hear and make sure there is no note the police might have missed. It's very fair of him. He's leaning over backward to give us a break, in fact. Not many cops would do that."

Bart swallowed whisky. He said, "I killed that girl, Marty. I scared her into doing this."

Land shook Hardin's shoulder. "Snap out of it," he said. "You're pretty sure she was a murderess who let a sick old man take the rap for her, who let him lie there in a stinking, hot little room with this thing on his mind, virtually under a death sentence. You say she set you up like a clay pigeon to be knocked off by her mobster friend. Don't get a guilt complex about this now. It's screwed up enough already."

"I'd think I was justified if she had left a note," Bart said. "But she didn't, you say, and that means her death serves no purpose. The fact that she committed suicide might be evidence enough for you and me that she was guilty, but it won't

91

be evidence enough for the cops and the D.A. It won't get
Lennox out of that little room."

"It can help, maybe," Marty said, but there was a false
note in his voice and Bart detected it.

"No," Bart said. "Suicide isn't a tacit admission of guilt,
not legally. Do you remember the Lindbergh case? A house-
maid who was connected with it committed suicide. She didn't
leave a note. So they tried Hauptmann just the same and sent
him to the electric chair. I've made another stupid blunder,
forcing her to do this. I knew she was unbalanced and was
capable of doing almost anything, but I put the pressure on
her just the same. So long as Elsa Travers was alive, we had a
chance. Now that she's dead, it seems our last hope is gone.
I've signed old Jim's death warrant."

"They've only made a cursory examination so far," Marty
said. "Something can break. I'm glad I didn't get undressed.
Let's get over there."

Bart followed Land into the hall. Land donned his floppy-
brimmed panama and picked up his malacca stick. They went
out into the night and found a cab.

The body still lay in the areaway, a blanket pulled over it.
A medical examiner had apparently just completed his examination and they were preparing the stretcher when Bart and
Marty arrived. Romano was among the policemen clustered
around the areaway.

He nodded toward the new arrivals, held up a hand to the
ambulance men. "Wait a minute," he said.

He turned to Marty. "It's not a pretty sight, counselor, but
I said you could see everything," he said. He pulled back the
blanket and Bart thought that the lieutenant had been right
when he said it was not a pretty sight. He noticed that Elsa
Travers was clad in the same matador slacks and silk sweater
she had been wearing earlier in the evening. But there was a
large silver pin on her breast that Bart had not noted before.
It was a curlicue design. Bart did not feel like moving close
enough to examine it.

Romano said, "This window was smashed by bullets earlier
tonight. The cops came here. It seemed like a pointless shooting because there was nobody in the areaway, or at least if
there was, he'd run off before anyone got here. Elsa hadn't
been home at the time of the shooting, Mrs. Mattingly said.
At least she wasn't in her room when the landlady roused the
house. It could have been some hopped-up young hoods who
were making like bad men on the television Late Late Show.

The shop was dark and there seemed no reason to shoot at it. We couldn't reach the proprietor of the shop right away because he'd just taken a shipment of costumes up to Sharon, Connecticut, so we left a patrolman on duty to guard the place until a new window could be put in or it could be boarded up."

He nodded toward a uniformed policeman. "Patrolman Hatton was on duty. He was standing on the sidewalk, right by the little fence. It was lucky he wasn't standing in the areaway. The body would have come right down on top of him. He could have been killed."

Land said, "I haven't any right to question you. Is there anything else you want to tell us, Lieutenant?"

"I'll tell you anything you want to know," Romano replied, "except there isn't much to tell. The slugs in the areaway were from a forty-five, another army gun, probably. Maybe that's significant. I wouldn't know. Either the shots or Mrs. Mattingly's screams brought out all the people in the house. Mrs. Mattingly and Montgomery and that magician Sandrean were here. Mrs. Mattingly said Elsa had made a phone call just a few minutes before, but that she wasn't in the house, apparently, when the shots were fired. That ventriloquist, Montgomery, and the magician, Sandrean, both were home. They couldn't tell the cops anything about the shots except they heard them and there was nobody there when they went outside. Patrolman Hatton saw Elsa come in and had her identify herself a little while later. Mrs. Mattingly told her what had happened and she says Elsa was terribly upset, almost hysterical. She went right up to her room. A little while later she jumped or fell off the roof. When Hatton waked them up to tell them what had happened and to phone in, they all came down again. Montgomery had been asleep. He was in his pajamas. Sandrean was still fully dressed. He said he saw Elsa going to the roof. He asked her where she was going and she told him she wanted some air. He offered to go up with her, but she told him off and said she didn't want his company. When Sandrean saw the body, he started sobbing and screaming and he ran away. Hatton was phoning in then and he couldn't stop him or even fire a warning shot. An alarm is out for Sandrean and a prowl car will probably be bringing him in soon."

"And there wasn't a note?" Land asked.

Romano said, "There was a note, but it wasn't a suicide note. It wasn't even written by Elsa. It was written by Sandrean. Come inside and I'll show it to you."

Hardin and Land followed the lieutenant to Elsa Travers'
room. Like the other rooms in the house, it was comfortably
furnished. A small book rack contained volumes dealing with
the meaning of dreams, a short treatise on reading tea leaves,
works on the astral and the occult. There were also books on
spiritualism by Lodge and Doyle and works on theosophy by
Annie Besant and Krishnamurti. Publicity stills of Elsa per-
forming various dance turns and one picture of her dancing
with Adrian Temple were tacked to the flowered wallpaper.

Romano opened the drawer to a desk and said, "We found
the note in here." He took a glassine envelope from his pocket.
He shook a folded piece of paper from the envelope to the top
of the desk. He opened the paper out carefully, using only the
nails of his thumbs and forefingers. He spread the paper on
the desk and said, "Fingerprints probably don't mean much,
but don't touch it anyway because it will be processed. Just
read it."

Bart and Marty bent over the outspread piece of writing
paper.

At the top, printed in bright red, was the figure of Satan in
full-dress clothes. He held a wand in one hand and the ace of
spades in the other. Also printed in red was the legend, EL
DIABLO, MAKER OF MIRACLES, *Member of the American Society of Magicians.* Down the right-hand side of the paper was
printed a long list of the theatres and clubs where Sandrean
had performed. The writing on the paper was in red ink and
it was the kind of writing that has not been taught in United
States schools for more than fifty years, a precise, shaded,
copperplate script. The message read:

Elsa:
Return the Feathered Serpent to me or destroy it. It can
bring only sorrow and evil and death. I was wrong to give
it to you.

                                              Sandrean

Land copied the message into a little leather-covered notebook. Romano returned the sheet of paper to the glassine
envelope and pocketed it.

Marty said, "Is there a man from the D.A.'s office here,
Lieutenant?"

Romano shook his head. "The D.A.'s office doesn't come
into a jumper case as a rule," he said.

"I submit that the death of Elsa Travers is closely connected with a case that does come under the discretion of the district attorney's office." Land said. "I submit that there is strong reason to believe that Elsa Travers was involved in the murder of Daphne Temple, or that she may at least have possessed guilty knowledge in connection with the murder, and that her suicide was the result of her connection with the murder of Daphne Temple. I suggest that this note and the flight of Sandrean make it reasonable to suppose that he himself was involved in the murder, along with Elsa Travers. I can produce a witness who will testify that Sandrean was in this house an hour before the murder was discovered. I submit that in view of all the facts I have stated, there are ample grounds for me to request the release from custody of my client, James Lennox."

Romano said, "I'm a cop. You can make your request to the D.A. tomorrow, or you can try to get a writ from a judge in view of the facts you've got. I can tell you what will happen, though. The D.A. won't take too much stock in your new facts because of the circumstantial evidence that still exists in the case of Lennox. And if you get a writ, he'll rush through an indictment for murder in the first degree in order to hold on to Lennox. The thing that interests me as a cop is that part about Sandrean. I didn't know he was in the house at the time you said he was."

"He was," Land replied. "He has admitted it."

"But he was at the Music Hall when the murder was committed," Romano commented. "Did he say why he was in the house? I'm like that poor King of England. Nobody ever tells me anything."

"He stated that he broke a set of dentures in his dressing room. He said he returned home for a spare set he had before his act went on. He said he tried to conceal this fact because it is embarrassing to him as a performer to have it known that he wears false teeth."

"I try to keep myself from jumping to conclusions, but if I heard a suspect tell a story like that, I'd jump to a conclusion," Romano said.

"What conclusion?" asked Marty .

"That the guy was telling the truth. You get to know a little something about psychology when you've been a cop as long as I have. When men and women tell lies and invent stories they don't invent stories that are embarrassing to themselves. You almost never find a guy trying to account for his time by saying he was passed out drunk somewhere, for instance. He'll claim he was at a picture show or something. When a man who's sensitive about wearing false teeth admits he wears them, you can be pretty sure he's innocent and he's telling the truth. If he was inventing a story, he'd have a different alibi entirely."

The patrolman named Hatton was at the door. He said, "A prowl car just rolled up, sir. They've picked up Sandrean. He was roaming around Broadway like he was in a daze, the cops say. They've got him downstairs now."

They went downstairs.

In the old-fashioned living room a husky young prowl-car cop stood beside the bedraggled little Mexican. The young cop said, "You want to take him, Lieutenant? We just got a Signal 32 on the talker. Citizens keep on acting up on a hot night like this."

"Where did you find him?" Romano asked.

"On Broadway, near Forty-fifth. He was just wandering around like he was drunk or in a daze. It wasn't hard to identify him with that trick mustache and goatee. He admitted who he was at once and didn't give us any trouble."

"Thanks," Romano said. "You can go on about your business. I'll take charge of him."

He turned to Sandrean, "Why did you run away?"

Sandrean said, "I don't know. They told me Elsa had jumped from the roof and when I saw here there, when I saw her poor broken body, the blood . . ." He began to sob.

Romano waited patiently. "I just ran," Sandrean said. "I didn't know where I was running. I ran until I had no more breath and then walked. I kept walking and presently this car came up and the officer said I was to go with them and they brought me here."

"When did you last see her alive?"

"A few minutes before it happened , before they called me to tell me she had jumped from the roof and killed herself. She came upstairs. I was sitting in my room, fully clothed, trying to read. My door was open for ventilation. I saw her start up the ladder and I went out to her. I noticed she was wearing the silver pin . She had never worn it before. I asked her what she was doing and she said she was going up for some air. She seemed terribly upset. I told her I would come up and talk to her , but she turned on me furiously and refused to permit it. I did not want to argue. Montgomery was sleeping in his room with the door ajar. He has been taunting me because of my love for Elsa. He has been making his foolish wooden dummy say terrible things to me. He was in love with Elsa, too, and he was jealous, I think. I did not wish to waken him. I went back to my room. Then there was a commotion just a few minutes later and Mrs. Mattingly was screaming. I ran downstairs. I saw Elsa there, dead, with the silver pin on her breast."

Romano took the note from the glassine envelope again, showed it to Sandrean. "Did you write this?" he asked.

Sandrean nodded dumbly. "I tried to get in touch with her today. She was not home when I was here. I came back between performances tonight to try to see her, even, but she was out again. So I wrote the note and put it beneath her door."

"What does the note mean? What is this crazy stuff about a feathered serpent?"

"It is not crazy. The first time that she wore it, the Feathered Serpent brought her death. Weeks ago, when I completed the Illusion of the Feathered Serpent for my engagement at the Music Hall, I was beside myself with happiness. It would give new life to my act, I thought. It had the elements of both mystery and humor. But I could not foresee what it would mean to mock an ancient god. I was so happy that I exhibited the illusion to Elsa before I even showed it to my agent. She was enthusiastic. There is a Mexican friend of mine who is a silversmith. He runs a little shop in Greenwich Village. I went down and had him make me a piece of jewelry, a little silver pin in the shape of the Feathered Serpent. I presented it to Elsa. Perhaps she knew that it was an evil omen. I do not know. But she never wore it. Not until tonight. And when she wore it, she died horribly."

Romano said, "I may want to talk to you again tomorrow, Sandrean. Here, maybe, or down at Manhattan West. I want you to be available."

Sandrean said, "I will be here. I will not run away again. You cannot run from the curse of ancient gods."

Bart and Land left the house with Romano. When the lieutenant had driven off in a police car, Bart said to Marty, "Are you going to try to persuade the D.A. to release Jim now? Are you going to ask a writ of habeas corpus?"

Marty shook his head. "I'm not too sure about the next move," he answered. "I was running a bluff and Romano knew it. I'm afraid we're more helpless now than we were before."

The first pearl glow of the false dawn was in the sky over Broadway. Marty studied it, said, "If I've read my Thoreau right and know my weather portents, it's going to be another hot one."

fourteen

The grizzled cop had fallen into a snorting sleep and looked as if he were about to tumble from the straight chair that was tilted beside the door of the little hospital room. The motherly-looking Negro nurse glanced down at him. Poor man, she thought, I hate to wake him up. She held a water pitcher of chipped enamelware in her hand. She shook the old cop gently.

As the cop gasped into sudden consciousnes, sweat broke out on his weatherbeaten face. A gray stubble had already begun to sprout on his flaccid jowls, although he had shaved just before he began his tour of duty.

The nurse said, "Sorry, but I've got to get inside. I go off duty in a little while and it's the rules I have to give them their wash before I do. I never could figure why you had to wake them up so early for their wash. I guess it's because the next shift has to give them breakfast."

The cop grunted and unlocked the door.

The old man lay on his back. His eyes were closed and his mouth was open. His lips were colorless, the same death-gray as his flesh. Breath wheezed through his open mouth.

The nurse got a pan, a towel and a washrag from beneath the bedside table. She pulled the sliding table up over the bed and laid a gentle hand on the old man's shoulder. His eyes flew open into staring, dazed wakefulness.

The nurse said, "Good morning! You get a little sleep in spite of the heat?"

The old man stared into her dark, kindly face. He said, "I—I don't know. I was dreaming. There was the clanging. I thought the clanging was important. I wanted to tell Bart."

"I know," the nurse said, "that clanging in the kitchens is a scandal. Enough to wake the dead. Let me give you a nice wash now."

She loosened the old man's gown and began to rub the wet, soapy rag over his frail body. "There's nothing to him at all," she told herself. "Just skin and bones, like a little boy that won't eat enough."

She dried the old man's body, sprinkled talcum on it. Then she washed his face. She poured cold drinking water from the bedside carafe over the rag and laid it on the old man's forehead. "There," she said. "Don't that feel good?"

The old man looked at her unbelievingly. "You're—you're good to me," he said.

They said the old man was a nasty murderer. He wasn't that to the nurse. He was just a patient, a poor, sick patient. She smiled down at him. "You're going to be all right," she said. "You're going to be just fine. Just you don't worry, now, you hear me?"

She finished and started for the door. The old man had the Look. She had seen the Look too many times. He had given up. Sometimes something happened to give them a new lease on life, to make them hope, but it wasn't going to happen with this old man, she was afraid. If it did, it better happen quick.

As the old cop locked the door after the nurse, he said, "How is he?" He didn't care how the old man was. He didn't give a damn. All he cared about was getting home and stripping himself naked and lying down on a bed with an electric fan blowing on him. But he thought he should say something.

The nurse shook her head. "He's not good," she said. "He's not good at all. He got the Look. And when they get the Look, they don't last long."

fifteen

Hardin had spent four sleepless hours in bed. Now, at a little after nine in the morning, he sat at a table in the Copper Skillet with a plate of ham and eggs in front of him and the morning papers piled beside the plate.

On the fifteenth day of the heat wave, the newspapers had suddenly decided to drop their flippant attitude. The heat was no longer something to joke about. People were dropping dead on the streets in alarming numbers. The city's sweltering tenements and overcrowded hospitals had become deathtraps. The poor who fled into the open spaces of the parks at night in the hope of finding air to breathe were the helpless prey of marauding hoodlums and psychopaths and even the augmented police force was insufficient to protect them. Crimes of violence always reached their highest peak in New York City in July and August, when the weather was hottest, and this year they set an all-time record along with the torrid temperatures.

The heat was still the headline in all papers, outranking war and murder and the baseball scores. But today the approach to it was different. There were no stale jokes about the sit-down strike of the Bermuda High. Editors had suddenly realized that the city's suffering millions did not find the heat wave humorous. There were no more gloating stories to the effect that the weather bureau could see no relief. The hard fact was that the temperature was expected to soar to 100 degrees officially today, for the first time in many years. That meant that it would be 107 or more in the shade of Times Square's tall buildings. The papers hinted that there was a vague possibility of rain in the late afternoon or evening. They tried to comfort the populace by pointing out that it was even worse in other parts of the country. Phoenix, Arizona, had hit a high of 116 the day before. The prairie towns of the Great Plains had baked under temperatures of more than 100 for four straight days and the heat in Chicago had been 2.8 degrees higher than that of New York.

The tabloids ran letters from readers who stated that the

heat was the delayed result of the atomic tests in the Arizona desert and at Bikini. One tabloid letter-writer dissented. He believed the heat wave was due entirely to flying saucers. He stated that the machines from outer space used a mysterious fuel that radiated heat waves one hundred times as far as hydrogen bombs and predicted the end of the world within six months. A more scholarly letter-writer in the New York Times, a meteorologist from Harvard University, stated that this was merely the culmination of a slow process that had been going forward for years and quoted a book he had written to prove it. He said that there was a shift of weather and that the Eastern Seaboard was becoming subtropical. To bolster his argument, he pointed out that a species of green crab, never seen before north of Florida, had appeared on Cape Cod and was ranging as far afield as Nova Scotia. The green crab, he said, was eating all the shrimp, much to the annoyance of the Cape Cod fisherman. In byline articles, medics and psychiatrists advised the populace to eat salt pills, which were unobtainable, and to relax, which was impossible.

The papers devoted some space to the suicide of Elsa Travers and to the bullet-smashed window of the costumer's shop, but even these happenings were tied in to the story of the heat wave. A tabloid grouped the two incidents together and headed its piece:

DANCER PLUNGES FROM ROOF; GUNMAN, CRAZY
WITH HEAT, SPRAYS LEAD AT MURDER HOUSE

Hardin finished his breakfast and left the stack of papers on the table. He found a cab and directed the driver to West Twentieth.

He found Romano in his little office at Manhattan West, lying on the leather couch and looking beat. Romano said, "I tried to catch some sleep here last night instead of going all the way up to the Bronx. My nervous duodenal is acting up again. I couldn't keep my breakfast down. And my blood pressure's jumping, too. But I guess you're tired of hearing me complain about my health. My wife says all I do is complain. She says I won't do anything about it, such as quitting the cops. She says it's being a cop that gives me blood pressure and a nervous duodenal. Maybe she's right. A guy I know just retired from the force and opened up a private agency and he wanted me to go in with him. But I don't see how I could be a private eye. I'm too old to have some dizzy blond

secretary sitting on my knee and I don't own a trench
coat and liquor makes my duodenal get more nervous."

"I want to see Jim Lennox at the hospital," Bart said.
"I came here to get whatever credentials are necessary."

Romano heaved himself to a sitting position and sighed
heavily. He rubbed his hand across his swarthy face and
smoothed his tangled hair.

"No one is supposed to see him but his lawyer and his
doctor or a member of the family," he said. "I guess maybe
you're the only family that he's got, so I can fix it for you to
get in. I'd take you down myself, but I'm so bushed that just
combing my hair's an effort. I'll peck you out a note on police
stationery. I wish Grierson was around. He usually does my
typing for me. That's the worst part about being a cop.
You've got to type things all the time."

He went to the battered desk and pulled the cover off
an equally battered typewriter. He took official stationery
from a drawer and put a sheet in the roller. He seated himself heavily and began to peck laboriously at the typewriter
with two fingers. He made several false starts and ripped the
paper from the typewriter and tossed it in the wastebasket,
.inserting a fresh sheet. It took him nearly ten minutes to
type out the brief note. Bart wondered how he ever managed the long reports he had to make. Maybe Grierson
handled them for him. Grierson was the new type of policeman and probably had a business-college education.

Romano insterted the sheet of paper in an envelope and
handed it to Bart. "This will get you in," he said, "but I
doubt they'll let you stay more than ten minutes or so."

Bart said, "Thanks," more curtly than he intended. The
old warm feeling for Romano had disappeared. Romano was
one of those who were callously letting an old man die in a
little room.

Hardin found an east-bound cab and directed the driver
to the old hospital on Twenty-ninth.

City was a sprawling structure behind a high brick wall
that covered four city blocks. The original Gothic buildings
had been constructed shortly after the Civil War, and many
wings, each of a different architectual period, had been added
through the years. The total effect was that of a builder's
bedlam. Medical men acclaimed City as a fine, progressive in-
stitution where important medical research was conducted,
but the place had an evil reputation because of its overcrowded and understaffed charity wards, its psychopathic and

alcoholic sections and, mainly, because it was the location of death's dread clearing house, the City Morgue.

There were grounds and a few trees inside the brick walls, but the grass was parched and the heat had withered the foliage of the trees to cornflake color. Bart entered the old Administration Building and, after losing himself in the twisting corridors several times, finally found the locked wards on the second floor. There was a prison-like iron gate that fenced off the entire section. A crisply laundered nurse sat at a small desk outside the gate. Bart handed her the note Romano had given him. She read it, said, "I'll have to show this to the police officer on duty. Wait here, please."

She went through the gate and locked it after her. She returned presently and handed the note to Bart. "You may go in," she said. "But you'll have to wait outside the door. The doctor is with the patient now."

Bart went through the gate and found a young policeman on duty outside Lennox's room. The policeman said, "I'll have to pat your pockets, mister. I hope you don't mind."

The policeman made a cursory examination of Bart's pockets. He said, "The doc went in a few minutes ago. He should be right out." As he finished speaking there was a tap on the door. The policeman unlocked it and young Dr. Bell, the intern, came out.

Bart said, "How is he, doctor?"

The doctor stared at Bart. "Who are you?" he asked fretfully.

"He's okay," the policeman said. "He's got police credentials."

The doctor said to Bart, "The main trouble is that he's old. That's something no doctor can do a thing about. You can't predict the reactions of a person his age to any particular physical or mental situation. They vary too widely in different cases. He has been in a state closely bordering on shock ever since he arrived. He shows no signs of snapping out of it, and there's nothing much we can do to bring him out of it. When they're in that state, they've simply lost the will to live and it's largely a psychiatric problem. Sometimes something happens to bring them out of it, and when it does, they get well almost immediately. Usually it's a mental stimulus. An old woman of eighty was dying in the same state up in the charity ward. There was no hope for her. Then her long-lost son suddenly appeared and she recovered completely in the time it takes to snap your fingers. Call it a miracle if you want to. That's about what it is, I guess. It's going to take a miracle, I'd say, to bring this old man out of it."

"If he learned that someone else had been arrested for this murder he's accused of, would that do it?" Bart asked.

"I think that's just about what it would take," the young intern answered. "But that would be a real miracle, wouldn't it? After all, there seems to be little doubt of his guilt."

The intern walked off toward the big ward, his stethoscope swinging from his neck.

The guard opened the door for Bart.

Hardin walked into the stifling, odorous heat of the tiny room.

The little man on the big bed sat bolt upright as Hardin entered and stared hard at him. His eyes had fever in them and they seemed enormous.

Suddenly the old man cried, "Bart! Bart!" Tears came into the staring eyes. "Have you come to take me home, Bart?"

Bart took a chair beside the bed and patted the old man's small hand. Brown freckles of age spotted the back of the hand.

Bart said, "Take it easy. We're going to get you out pretty quick now. The cops think they're on the trail of the real murderer and the case can break wide open any minute. You just have to be patient for a little while."

"Bart, do they really believe I'm a murderer? Does Lieutenant Romano believe that? I've known Lieutenant Romano for so long. He used to walk a beat on Broadway years ago. I knew him then. Does he believe I'm a murderer, Bart?"

"Of course he doesn't," Bart said. "It's just that you're an important witness because you happened to be standing there on the fire escape. Romano is going to close in on the real murderer, I tell you. He just has to hold you here until he does."

"But it's so hot in here, Bart, and it's like being in jail. They lock the door and there's a policeman right outside all the time. I wouldn't run away. I haven't any place to go."

The effort seemed to have exhausted Lennox. He fell back on the pillow. Bart sat and patted his hand. He could think of nothing else to do.

Lennox spoke again. His voice seemed to have grown weaker. He said, "Bart, I thought of something I wanted to tell you. It comes to my mind and then I can't remember

what it is. I thought of it last night, or maybe it was the night
before. I can't keep track of time. The hours drag by so
slowly. It had something to do with a noise, a sound, I
think. I asked them to call you before I forgot, but they
didn't. I think it was important."

"Try to remember," Bart urged.

The old man pushed himself up to a sitting position
again. "I do, Bart!" he cried. "I do remember! They were
clattering pots and pans around in the kitchen underneath me
and it reminded me of another sound, a metallic sound that
I had heard the night of the murder, a second after the shot
was fired. I thought of what it must have been! The murderer threw his gun away and it hit on the platform of the
fire escape. If I heard the murderer throw the gun away, I
couldn't possibly have killed her, could I? Will that help,
Bart? Will it help Lieutenant Romano to find the one who's
really guilty?"

Bart sat for a minute, squeezing the old man's hand, his
face hard. It was almost incredible that he could be so
naïve, that he could believe they would take the word of
a suspected murderer for a thing like that. But he obviously
did believe it. For a moment his old face was almost radiant.
Maybe it would help him to hang on for a little while.

Bart said, "Jim, that's wonderful! It may be just what
Romano needs, the missing piece. I'll tell him right away and
we'll have you out of here quicker than you expect, even."

"I hope so, Bart. I can't stand this mental torture much
longer. And this heat, it's awful, awful."

Bart said, "I'm going out now and I'm going to bring
you back an electric fan. That'll help some until Romano
is able to clear this whole thing up."

The old man looked at Bart with a curious expression. He
said, "I'm not sure, Bart. I think you may be humoring me
as if I were a child. Maybe the thing I remembered has no
real importance."

"Of course it has," Bart declared, and hoped his voice
sounded convincing. "You keep your chin up, Jim. I'll be
right back with the electric fan. Then I'll go see Romano."

As the policeman closed and locked the door, Bart said,
"It's all right if I come back, isn't it? I want to bring the old
man something."

The cop looked dubious. "I don't know," he answered. "I
guess it's all right if the hospital people okay it. I could
take him in some ice cream or something, I suppose."

Bart said, "Thanks. I'll be right back."

He found an electric shop on Twenty-ninth Street.

The proprietor said, "You're lucky. They're short of electric fans all over New York. You can't get 'em for love or money since the heat wave started. But I managed to get just half a dozen in this morning. I've already sold three to regular customers."

He showed Bart a medium-sized fan, said, "It's a three-speed, oscillating job. Fine a fan as you can find. The list price is seventeen-fifty and I could get twice that if I put it on the black market. I've been selling rebuilt jobs for more."

Bart took the fan and paid for it. He told the salesman not to bother wrapping it. He carried the fan back to the hospital.

The nurse on the locked ward stopped him. She said, "Where do you think you're going with that, mister?"

Bart said, "I'm taking it to Mr. Lennox. That little room is horribly hot."

"Every place is horribly hot on a day when the temperature is a hundred," the nurse replied acidly. "I can't permit you to take that fan in, I'm afraid."

"Why?" asked Bart, anger coming into his face. "Are you suppose to see he suffers as much as possible?"

The nurse's voice had become hard and professional. "There are psychopathic cases in this section, sir," she said. "We can't take a chance on a patient doing himself some injury. The whirling, metal blade of an electric fan can be dangerous to anyone with suicidal tendencies. I can't give you permission to take the fan in. That's final."

"Who can give me permission?"

"I can call the floor nurse if you wish me to."

"Please call her," Bart said.

The floor nurse was a prim, middle-aged woman with a black band around her cap. She wore gold-rimmed eyeglasses.

She said, "What is the difficulty, please?"

The ward nurse explained. The floor nurse shook her head at Bart. "It's quite impossible," she said.

"Look," said Bart, "Mr. Lennox isn't a psychopathic case. They put him here because he has a heart condition. He isn't going to try to cut his wrists on an electric fan."

The floor nurse shrugged. "I'm sorry, sir. He is accused of murdering a young girl, you know. That might indicate he is violent, certainly."

Young Dr. Bell, the intern, was passing. The floor nurse called him and explained the situation.

Dr. Bell said, "I couldn't possibly permit a fan in that ₁ᴜᴜm. No."

"Why?" demanded Bart. "Just because you're cruel and stupid?"

Dr. Bell bridled. "You are discourteous and you don't deserve an explanation," he said. "But I will give you one. It isn't only the chance that he may inflict self-injury. Old people come here with many ailments—heart trouble, broken hips, arthritis. They seldom die from those. Most of them die from two main causes—uremia and pneumonia. I can't take a chance on the breeze from an electric fan giving a perspiring patient pneumonia, and I won't."

There was the fury of exasperation in Bart's face now. A large metal trash can stood nearby. Bart hurled the electric fan into the trash can. There were glass bottles in the can and the smash was resounding.

The floor nurse glared at him through her gold-rimmed glasses. "We should lock you up here!" she flared. "You're crazier than any of the patients in the psychopathic ward!"

sixteen

Dr. Pellman, the psychiatrist, was a tall, guant man. He was making his morning round of the Big Ward, the dreaded Ward 80, now. You had to thread your way carefully. There were seventy-six beds in the ward that had been meant to hold only forty-five. The beds were head to foot all down the middle of the long aisle. Dr. Pellman glanced at charts and occasionally spoke to a patient. Many of the patients just lay on their backs and stared fixedly at the cracks in the plaster ceiling. Some sat on the edge of the bed and mumbled to themselves. A few looked too bright, too alert. Manic depressives who were approaching the stage of extreme excitement, Dr. Pellman thought.

He looked at a bed tag, said to a fat and bleary-eyed old man, "This is your fourth trip here in the last year, Murphy. Do you feel better today? Do you want to get out so you can get drunk all over again?"

The old man said, "They didn't give me no paraldehyde today, doc. They didn't even give me a goof ball to make me sleep last night. I've got the shakes something awful. The fillings are coming out of my teeth."

"You'll get over them, Murphy. You can't rely on drugs forever," the doctor said, passing on to the next bed.

He looked at the young man on the bed. He said, "Ah, Temple. I want to see you in the office as soon as I'm through in here. Tell the nurse."

As the doctor moved on, Murphy leaned over toward the young man in the next bed. "Hey, you know what that means?" he asked. "It means they're bugging you. It means you're going out to Rockland or Islip, that's what it means. They throw the key away when they put you there, boy."

Temple didn't answer. When the doctor had finished his rounds, he got up off the bed, put on a hospital robe and walked the length of the ward to the little office.

Dr. Pellman said, "Sit down, Temple. I want to talk to you. Did you know you're going home this afternoon? In just a few hours now?"

Adrian Temple said, "I didn't know that, sir."

109

"There seems to be no reason to hold you longer. Your wife's funeral is tomorrow, I understand. The police don't wish to put a hold on you. And our examination reveals no reason for commitment. You're highly neurotic. That's part of the artistic temperament, I suppose. You are either an alcoholic already or you're on the verge of becoming one. You have a morbid fear of physical pain that amounts to phobia. But none of that constitutes legal or medical insanity. There's one thing that disturbs me very much, however. Something you haven't heard about. I thing I should break the news to you." He consulted some notes, said, "This dancing partner of yours, Elsa Travers, the one who lived in the same rooming house with you. She committed suicide last night."

Temple said, "Oh, my God, no! Why? Did she leave a note, give a reason?"

Dr. Pellman shook his head. "Not that I know of," he said. "She apparently just went up to the roof and jumped off. Her death was instantaneous. Perhaps this murder had just preyed on her mind. She was an odd, highly sensitive person, it seems. Do you think her death is going to have a bad effect on you? Do you think it will give you more delusions about murdering people?"

"I know I couldn't have murdered her," Temple answered softly. "I know that. I've been fully conscious of what's happened since I've been here."

"Do you still think you killed your wife, Adrian?" The doctor had reached the sympathetic, understanding stage of the interview now. He always used the patient's first name at this point.

"I guess I couldn't have," Temple answered, wiping perspiration from his forehead. "But I can't believe that nice old man did it, either. It just doesn't seem possible. He was so good to Daphne. He sat with her by the hour and read to her and kept her company."

"Nice old men go berserk during heat waves like anybody else," the doctor said. "But what about you? Are you still laboring under the delusion you killed your wife?"

"The impression is still strong, but of course I was drunk. I often imagine things when I am drinking. I suppose the suicide pact we had implanted the idea in my mind."

"You don't think you're likely to get drunk again and go to the police and confess another murder, do you? It might go hard with you the next time. You might be committed. And that's not pleasant."

"I can't imagine that I will. I think the other times it was the suicide pact working on my mind. I knew my poor wife wanted to die. I had promised her I would go through with it, but I never could. I think when I was drunk those times I imagined the murders as a sort of compensation for my failure to keep the bargain."

"That's remarkably sound psychology for a layman, Adrian," Dr. Pellman said. "Now tell me how you have felt while you were here, tell me what things have come in to your mind these past hours."

Temple looked down at the floor. "I—I hate to have to confess it," he said. "But I've hardly grieved at all over my wife's death, not the way I should have. I don't even feel hatred toward the man who murdered her. I guess I've been in a morbid state, though, because I've been worrying about myself, about suffering pain. One of the men in the ward described shock treatment to me. I was so afraid they would give me that. I didn't think I could stand it. And they stuck needles into another man and he screamed. I was afraid every time a nurse came in because I thought she was going to stick a needle in me." Temple shuddered.

"In a way, that's a healthy sign. You've accepted your wife's death and you're not brooding over it. Oddly enough, complete selfishness is sometimes the best indication of recovery in a case like this," the doctor said. "Of course this fear of pain is definitely a psychosis. It's the thing that places you on the border line between a neurotic and a psychotic. It's unquestionably a trauma that dates from your childhood. It would take long months of analysis to bring it out, and unfortunately we don't have time for that. If you can afford a private analyst, I would advise it. If not, you might try the psychiatric clinic. Your drinking is something you can do something about. Try Alcoholics Anonymous. Get some hobbies. It's very dangerous for you to drink. Do you think you can stay away from liquor, Adrian?"

Temple shrugged. "I honestly don't know," he said. "With my wife gone and my dancing partner gone, there's not much but liquor left for me, is there?"

The psychiatrist's eyes followed Temple's slender figure as the ward patient walked out of the office. Dr. Pellman shook his head. It was a shame to discharge them when they were in a state like that, but he had to do it every day. There was simply no room for them. Psychotics and neurotics were temporarily lodged in wards for the city's sick in hospitals all over town because there was no room for them here where they belonged. They needed the beds. It used to be that they kept them a minimum of five days. Then it had gone down to three. Now they got them out even faster if it was humanly possible, rushing through the fundamental tests in a twenty-four-hour period sometimes, especially in police cases. Unless they were violent, their stay at City was a short one, often only overnight. With the chronic alcoholics the situation was even worse. They didn't even let them past the admittance office unless it was absolutely necessary. They gave them a spoonful of paraldehyde to steady them long enough to reach the subway, and that was sometimes all the treatment they received.

Temple wasn't mad. Where was the border line between the neurotic and the psychotic? the doctor asked himself. Somebody had said that the neurotic built dream castles and the psychotic lived in them. Temple had lived in a bad dream, for a little while. He had been sure he had killed his wife. But according to all the tests, Temple was not insane. Still, he needed help and the doctor had no help to offer him because there wasn't enough space to keep the patients, there weren't enough beds or places to put the beds. It was even worse in this heat wave. Some day, he thought, I'll do a monograph on the relation of weather to the unstable personality.

Dr. Pellman glanced briefly at the folder with Temple's name on it as he slammed a rubber stamp on the papers inside it. Adrian Temple had become a number in a file index. Dr. Pellman dismissed the patient from his mind.

The doctor sighed and took an aspirin tablet for his headache.

seventeen

Hardin walked west blindly on Twenty-ninth Street. He was walking fast despite the heat. He had no immediate destination in mind. He was trying to walk off the crazy fit of anger, the sense of complete futility he had experienced in the hospital. He had almost reached the flagstoned paths of the Little Church Around the Corner when he noticed an old, sedate hotel building. The sign stated that it was for women only. On an impulse, Hardin turned into the hotel.

The lobby was paneled with old wood that badly needed refinishing. The upholstery of the chairs and settees was threadbare. Dusty plants were potted in urns of Della Robbia ware. Hardin went to the desk, picked up a house phone and asked for Alma Turner.

The fortuneteller said, "Mr. Hardin! I'm almost frantic. I tried to reach you at your office and your home. Please wait. I'll be right down."

It took five minutes for her to reach the lobby. She apologized for the brief delay and explained that the elevator service was slow because the man who ran it was also the bellboy and the room-service waiter. She led Hardin into a small writing room off the lobby. It was deserted at this hour.

"I'm simply shaken, Mr. Hardin," Alma Turner said. "Nothing has ever hit me as hard as this. I didn't know about it until about an hour or so ago, when they brought up my morning paper. I was having my coffee when I saw the story about that girl committing suicide and I got sick all over. I felt that I had sent her to her death, frightened her into doing this awful thing. I admit this silly fortunetelling business of mine is slightly illegal, but no one has ever been hurt by it before. I like to think it's even made their dull lives more bearable for most of the girls who come to me. And now this has happened. I'm simply beside myself."

Hardin said, "If anyone's to blame, it's not you. The full responsibility is mine. I'm going to tell you something. That girl tried to have me killed last night. She had a gunman who was her boy friend empty his gun at me and it's a

113

miracle I'm alive. I'm absolutely sure she could have got old Jim Lennox cleared in this business if she had told the truth. Instead, she just left him dying of a kind of cancer of the spirit. The only chance we had to save Lennox was to force her out in the open. What you told her accomplished that. Only it didn't work out the way I thought it would. She tried to get me killed, and when she failed, she killed herself."

"Still, I am responsible, Mr. Hardin. I told her those awful things. I should have anticipated the reaction of a person who was already as emotionally upset as she was. I can't pretend I liked her. She gave me the creeps, in fact. I felt that she was sick, in an evil sort of way. But I would never, never have wanted a horrible thing like this to happen."

"You couldn't foresee it would happen," Bart said. "You did exactly what I told you to and your motive was the best in the world. You were trying to help an innocent old man. Think about it that way. And there's still a chance that what we did can help Jim. It's about the only chance, in fact."

"I hope so," Alma said. "I hope some good can come out of all this evil."

"I want you to tell me just what happened when she came to the tearoom," Bart said.

"She must have come on the run after I called her. I told her I had been gazing in my crystal ball and I kept seeing the clouded image of her face, and that I could see she was in deep, deep trouble. I told her I wanted to read the leaves and tell her fortune with the cards. I pretended to see a gallows form, a symbol of violence and murder and death, in the leaves. I've learned to do some conjurer's tricks with cards. You have to, in my business. I always try to palm the ace of spades, the death card, or I leave it out of the deck entirely because some of my clients read books on fortune-telling and know what it means and I don't want it to come up. And since I usually want to bring a strange man into their lives, I've learned to extract the jacks from almost any place in the deck, especially the jack of hearts. Last night I produced the ace of spades and a red and black jack when I told Elsa's fortune. The red jack was you and the other was this dark and evil man you wanted me to describe. I went from the cards to the crystal and I was on safe ground there, because I could go into a pretty accurate description of you and she had no way of checking me. It was obvious she recognized you at once. I told her that the other man knew

something about her and that you had found it out and that
it was connected with death and murder and the gallows.
That was enough. She got as white as death. I was really
afraid she was going to faint. Then she asked me if I knew
Bart Hardin. I said I didn't."

Hardin's eyes narrowed and he thought a minute. Finally
he said, "That means she might have suspected there was
collusion between us, that I had tipped you off to tell her
that I knew a damaging fact about her that was connected
with the murder of Daphne Temple."

"It's possible," Alma Turner answered. "I wouldn't even
try to guess what might be going on in the mixed-up mind of
a person like Elsa Travers. It's also possible that she actually
believed I saw it all in the tea leaves and the cards and the
crystal ball."

"Anyway, she took action pretty quickly," Bart said. "She
persuaded the 'dark, mysterious man' to try to murder me."

Alma said, "When she left, she was almost in a trance.
She hurried off as if she had some urgent errand, something
that couldn't wait."

"I want to try to relieve your mind," Hardin said. "Maybe
I also want to try to justify myself. On accout of Jim Lennox,
we had to force that woman's hand last night. We couldn't
foresee what would happen. Think of it this way. It's more
than likely that she murdered Daphne Temple. She certainly
tried to have me murdered. And she was perfectly willing to
see an old man accused of a dreadful crime and to keep her
mouth shut even though she knew that shock was slowly
killing him. We can't feel too guilty about what we did under
the circumstances."

"I—I think maybe I feel a little better," Alma replied.
"But I'm afraid I'll never have quite the same attitude toward
the business that I'm in, my racket, if you want to call it that.
Up to now, it's just seemed an easy, fairly pleasant way for an
old lady to make a living in this big, tough town. But now
the tea leaves and the cards and all the trappings aren't just
silly playthings. They seem evil. Maybe I'm getting as crazy as
my customers."

Hardin rose and said, "I've got to go now. I've got a lot
of things to do today. If I don't get Jim Lennox out of that
little room, I'm afraid he's coming out in a box."

He left the old hotel and found a cab near Fifth Avenue.
He directed the driver to the Broadway Times.

The cab turned west on Forty-ninth Street. As it headed

into Jacobs Beach, Hardin saw a big black Cadillac with a uniformed chauffeur pulling away from the curbing in front of Moe Selig's bookie shop. Bart glanced at his watch. It was just eleven-thirty. Selig was early today. He usually did not arrive at his place of business until after lunch.

Bart said to the heap jockey, "Signals over. I'll jump out here."

He paid the cab and entered the cigar store that was the front for Selig's gambling rooms. Eddie O'Grady, the Old Top Sarge, was already on duty as lookout behind the cigar counter with its dummy boxes and cartons. Hardin said, "Did Selig come in?"

"He just blew in, Captain. He's in his office. There's been action for a certain horse in the third at Aqueduct ever since early this morning, big action. Selig thinks the boys have fixed themselves up a boat race and he don't want the book to get hit. He wants to make sure all the bets are laid off at the track. He's in there with his lay-off men."

Bart said, "I want to see him."

The Old Sarge nodded. He came from behind the counter and opened the door to the horse room. There were few customers at this time of day. The rush began after noon. Sheet-writers and block men were setting up. A few horse-players were sitting at long tables studying the past-performance sheets from the *Broadway Times* and the Armstrong scratch sheets. Selig stood in the middle of the big room, talking earnestly to three hard-looking men.

Selig was saying, "They ain't no use in laying it off with other books in the Syndicate or even the louse books that are outside it. They're betting on this one in China. St. Louis and Chicago are already calling in for us to lay off the overload at the track for them. This bum is four to one and your money back in the morning line. We'll throw it all into the machines and beat the odds down to even money or maybe odds-on and see how the suckers like the pay-off. I'd like to know who made this fix without telling Selig."

He turned to a hulking man beside him, said, "Artie, you stay in that candy store outside the track, right by the pay phone. I own the candy store, so there won't be trouble. We'll phone in the late bets to you if they're big enough to bother with. Joe, you stand outside the track, right outside the gate. Wait till the last minute and get the signal of how much from Artie. Monk, you're inside. Right inside. You get the word from Joe and you run like hell to the windows. I'll have a couple of more men with you to spread it out. I'll cut the bets on the third off here ten minutes before post no matter how loud they squeal. They ain't dumping coarse notes on a boat race to Selig a couple of minutes before they're off."

Selig shook his head. "And you know what'll happen?" he said. "This bum that's all fixed to win will fall over the fence or get beat somehow and we'll have laid off all that nice, fresh money instead of keeping it. It always happens that way. But Selig can't take a chance. Selig ain't a gambler. He's a businessman."

The field marshal, having issued his grand strategy to his lieutenants, strode into his little office. Hardin followed him.

Selig said, "Hello, editor. You got up before your breakfast. You here to make a borrow? Don't tell me you've blown all that cabbage you picked up in the floater just a night or two ago."

Bart said, "I want to hire some muscle."

"You?" Selig said, pretending wide-eyed surprise. "Why, editor, I always thought you was a big, tough ex-Marine or something. You mean you need a bodyguard?"

"Maybe," Bart answered. "Your boy Stony threw a little lead at me last night."

Selig grinned and ran his tongue over his yellowed upper teeth. "Was that before or after you put the boot in his face, editor?"

"Before," Bart replied. "So you heard about it."

"Selig hears a lot of things. Hearing things is part of Selig's business. Don't worry about Stony, editor. It's taken care of. He's been talked to, and when a punk like Stony gets talked to by the right people, he listens."

"I'm not worried. But I want to hire some muscle."

Selig's eyes narrowed. "You want a gun?" he asked. "I know some guns who are unemployed. There's not much work for them nowadays. Too much competition from the amateurs."

"I don't want a gun. I just want some muscle. Some big, ugly muscle."

Selig grinned. "Maybe I got the man for you. He just come in from Chi. He had a bad rap there and he's on vacation and I don't know what to do with him. You'd like him, editor. Mr. Wilson is his name. He's big and ugly, but he's a gentleman. A college man, no kidding. He played football at a real honest-to-God college. And he's a hero. What's it they call those commando guys? Rangers, that's it. Mr. Wilson was a Ranger in the war. He's got medals to prove it. Mr. Wilson don't pack a gun. That's against the law, I understand. Mr. Wilson uses a little piece of wire. He says he learned about the wire in the Rangers. He showed me how it works. He says you slip up behind a guy and put the wire around his neck and kinda twist and jerk at the same time. Mr. Wilson claims sometimes the guy's head comes off his shoulders if you do it just right. He's very proud of that little piece of wire, Mr. Wilson is. Like a doll with a new mink coat."

Selig leaned back in his swivel chair and put bowed legs on his desk. "Don't Mr. Wilson sound nice, editor? He'd come cheap, too, because he's unemployed right now. A college boy. A soldier and a gentleman. Real class. He should be just your type."

Hardin said, "I don't want Mr. Wilson and his wire. I just want muscle. I want Stony Martin."

Heavy lids veiled Selig's eyes. He said, "Oh-oh, editor. Now you're getting me irritated. I wasn't going to mention it, but I didn't like what you did last night. I tried to help you out and help the old man out and you went and loused things up, but good. You made a damned dumb dame jump off a roof and that could be trouble. And it wasn't nice to kick poor Stony's face in. He's been belted so many times already he can't tell you what time it is when he's looking at a clock. Let it lie, editor. Forget about Stony. I told you he's been talked to."

"I'm not mad at him," Bart replied. "I just want to hire him. I'll pay whatever rates you get for muscle."

"What do you want with him?"

"I want him to be at a certain place at a certain time."

"A certain place where a safe will fall on his head, maybe?"

"He won't get hurt," Bart answered. "At least I won't hurt him. It's just a job."

Selig thought about it.

At length he said, "What place, what time?"

"My flat. At six tonight."

Selig said, "Stony ain't worth much doing anything for anybody. Just leave a couple of C-notes on the desk. It's a contribution for the Old Bookmakers' Home."

Bart put the money on Selig's desk. He said, "You'll have him there at six for sure?"

"Stony walks on his heels from taking too many on the chin and his brains have got soft-boiled, but he still knows enough to go where Selig tells him," the mobster answered. "But don't let any safes land on Stony's head. That might get Selig kind of irritated."

eighteen

Hardin walked from the horse room to the *Broadway Times*, although he had no intention of working that afternoon. He had more important matters on his mind than putting out a newspaper.

As he entered the old building, Bertha, the phone girl, said, "There's a lady waiting in your office, boss. She says you're going to put her picture in the paper."

Bart did not go to his little cubicle immediately. He stopped at the horseshoe copy desk where Pops Taylor was sitting in the slot making marks on copy paper. Hardin said, "Pops, it's the worst heat wave in New York history and it's the height of the racing season. You're turf editor and you're swamped with work. You're going to have to do more work today. I'm taking off. Can you handle the act?"

Pops looked up at Hardin over his half-moon glasses. "According to the rumbles around the Street there's a real fuzzy going today in that third at Aqueduct," he said.

"I heard about it," Bart replied. "Moe Selig is laying off all he's holding at the track. It'll wind up two to five."

"That's the trouble with fuzzies," Pops said. "They wind up at the eighth pole or they wind up two to five. After forty years on this blat I can handle any act so long as there's a little ammunition in back of Volume 9. Have fun." He returned to his copyreading.

Bart grinned. "If the ammunition gives out, replenish it," he said. "Charge a bottle to me at the liquor store. I'm going to try to get Jim Lennox out of that hospital today, Pops."

Pops cocked one eye up at Hardin over the crescent lens. "Do you think you can?" he asked. "I might even be willing to work without the ammunition to help you do that, son."

"I'm going to try," Bart said. "I'm going to make a college try. My time is giving out, Pops."

"So is Lennox's," Pops commented. "When you get old you don't have too much time to waste."

Bart walked into his office. Chloe Fields was perched on

120

Bart's swivel chair, with her legs crossed. Her thin print skirt had crawled up high above her shapely knee. She was apparently having a conversation with Orville Cartwright, the six-foot, teen-age copy boy. Chloe was saying, "You sure are big for your age. I kind of go for red-headed boys. Red-headed boys are so—fiery."

Orville's inner fires were burning in his immature face. He was blushing furiously. He left hurriedly as Hardin entered.

Hardin said, "Hello, Chloe. Don't tell me you've had the pictures taken already."

"I found an old picture I forgot I had," Chloe replied. "I've got lots of clothes on in it. Once when things were tough I did some modeling for a furrier."

She took an eight-by-ten glossy print from an envelope and handed it to Bart. He looked at it and laughed. Little Chloe was swathed from neck to ankles in a voluminous fur wrap. She even wore a fur hat over her blonde hair.

Bart said, "You look like a cross between Davy Crockett and a Russian droshky driver. You're the damnedest gal I ever knew. You're either in bare skin or bearskin, spelt differently. Look, kid, what I want is a picture that shows enough of Chloe to make it interesting, but not enough to get the paper banned from the U. S. mails. You must have some costume that's more than a bangle and less than a fur rug. If I ran this during the heat wave, more people would start dying on the streets."

Chloe bit her lip. "Gee," she said. "I was hoping I wouldn't have to pay to have another picture taken. I wanted to keep that fifty bucks I blackmailed out of you. I need it."

"Keep it," Bart said. "You go home and find some costume that's a compromise between formal dress at a nudist camp and the latest fashions at a Quaker prayer meeting and I'll have our own photographer make the shot."

"I could wear my practice rompers," Chloe said. "They're kind of cute. They've got polka dots."

"That should be just fine," Bart said. He picked up the phone and spoke to Pete Cruise, the paper's photographer. He told him a girl named Chloe Fields was coming in later to have her picture taken. Cruise inquired the reason for making the picture.

"We'll think up an angle," Bart said. "Maybe we'll elect her Miss Heat Wave."

He turned to Chloe and said, "It's all set. Come back this afternoon and our photographer, Pete Cruise, will be expecting you."

"What kind of fellow is he?" Chloe asked.

Bart said, "He's a hard-bitten, sour-faced mug who's been taking pictures of showgirls and race horses so long he can't tell 'em apart. You've got nothing to worry about. Come on. I'll walk you home and you can get your rompers. It's too hot to work."

"Oh-oh," Chloe said. "This guy believes in collecting in advance."

Bart said, "Don't worry, sugar. There won't be a pay-off. I've got other things on my mind today. I'm going to that theatrical rooming house next door to you."

Hardin and Chloe walked through the heat to Fifty-third Street. The girl jabbered all the way, but Hardin hardly heard her. His mind was on a murdered girl and an old man in a little room.

He said good-by to Chloe at the entrance to Mrs. Mattingly's house. He noticed that the front of the costumer's shop had been boarded up.

Chloe said, "Can't you come up for just a minute? I want you to see if the rompers are all right."

Bart grinned as he saw the girl's earnest face. This trivial matter was of utmost importance to her. He glanced at his watch. The noon hour was only half gone. It would be more than five and a half hours before the showdown came. He had plenty of time.

He accompanied Chloe to her studio apartment.

A gossamer brassière and a pair of panties had been thrown carelessly on the couch. Chloe grabbed them and said, "I wasn't expecting visitors."

She unzipped a pillow cover and stuffed the panties and brassière inside it. She said, "That's what I like about zipper pillow covers. You can hide things inside them."

Bart stood stock still for a moment, staring at the pillow. His face was set in rigid lines.

Chloe looked at him in amazement. "Say!" she said. "What's the matter with you? Do a few little old undies shock you that bad, mister?"

Bart said, "Chloe, I think you just solved a murder."

Chloe stared at Bart with wide eyes. "Me?" she said. "Little old Chloe?"

Bart patted her shoulder. "Skip it, sugar," he said. "Let's see the rompers. I've got to get out of here."

Chloe went to a drawer and, after a brief search during which several stockings and other garments spilled to the floor, found what she was after. She carried the rompers toward the bathroom and said, "Don't go away, now. I'll be right out."

She came out presently clad in the rompers. They would pass the censors—just, Bart thought.

A stridulous voice resounded from the house next door.

"Hello, there, cutie! Where'd you get the pretty rompers? Is that Mr. Hardin there with you?"

Chloe and Bart went to the window. Woodenhead Willie, the ventriloquist's dummy, was perched on the window sill of a third-floor room in the Mattingly house and he was flapping his wooden jaws busily. Montgomery must have been stooping down beside him, out of sight. The jaunty Willie waved a wooden arm at Bart. "Hi, there, Hardin!" he called. "I see you finally figured out what was in that little hole in the wall. Have you thought about poor Elsa? Do you realize somebody might have *pushed* her off that roof?"

The window to Sandrean's room next door suddenly slammed shut, and a shade was pulled over it. Woodenhead Willie cackled with laughter.

"I like your rompers, cutie," he called. "Come up and see me sometime."

Chloe shook her head. "It's not enough I've got those two crazy characters peeping at me all the time," she said. "Now I've got a wooden dummy watching everything I do."

Bart said, "Go back to the office and get your picture taken. I've got to leave."

As he started out of the room, Chloe called, "Mister . . ."

Bart turned. Chloe said, "You're kind of big and tough, mister, but you know something? You're real sweet in a way."

Bart closed the door and went to the Mattingly house. Dora answered the bell and told him Mrs. Mattingly was in the living room. He found her sitting on the couch. She was clad in the feathered negligee and she was waving an old-fashioned palm-leaf fan in front of her face.

Bart said, "I understand Temple is coming home today."

Mrs. Mattingly nodded. "I called the hospital," she said. "I thought someone should meet the poor man, he's been through so much. And there's danger he might go on another spree if he's all alone at a time like this. He's being released late this afternoon. Mr. Montgomery has kindly offered to go down for him. This heat and these horrible happenings in the house have unnerved me to the point that I'm simply not up to it."

"I have to ask one more favor," Bart said. "I want to see that room once more before Temple comes home."

"There's no objection now," Mrs. Mattingly replied. "I talked to the police and asked permission to clean the room before Adrian comes back. They're through in there. They've examined everything and taken photographs. And thank goodness they've taken that wheelchair of Daphne's with them. I suppose they want it because of the bullet hole in the frame. It would be too grim a reminder for Adrian if he came home and found it standing there vacant. I was going to take it out myself if the police hadn't done so. Dora's just cleaned the room. It isn't locked. You can go up, but please don't muss it up."

Bart said, "I won't."

He went to the hall and mounted the stairs. He went into the room and closed the door behind him. He disregarded the big bed on which Daphne Temple had slept. He went immediately to the small studio couch. He began to pat the three pillows that were encased in zippered corduroy slips. Two were firmly filled, their contours squared off. The other had looser stuffing. It was soft to the touch. Bart unzipped the pillow. As the air was released by the opened cover a little white feather floated out. Bart did not remove the cover. He looked inside and saw that a pillow with striped ticking, a pillow that did not fit the case, had been inserted in it. It was stuffed with feathers, white feathers. Bart could see the feathers, because many of them had spilled out of a large charred hole in the ticking.

Bart zipped the cover shut and picked up the feathers that had drifted out onto the bedspread. He rolled the feathers into a little ball with his thumb and forefinger. He dropped them into a wastebasket.

There was no doubt now.

He knew how Daphne Temple had been killed and he knew her murderer.

He walked out of the room and closed the door.

The young ventriloquist, Montgomery, was standing at the foot of the third-floor stairs. He held his dummy in his arm. The dummy's jaws began to clack. He said, "Doesn't that

Mr. Hardin get around, Charlie? Here he is again. But he hasn't got that cutie in the rompers with him."

Bart said, "Don't you ever say anything yourself, Montgomery? Does your dummy do all the talking?"

"Oh, I talk sometimes," Montgomery answered. "But I prefer to have Woodenhead Willie speak for me. I'm not responsible for what Woodenhead Willie says, you see."

"I'd like to ask a few questions," Bart said, "and I'd like to have you answer them in person. Willie's voice kind of grates on me."

"Oh, that nasty man!" Woodenhead Willie exclaimed. "He doesn't like my dulcet baritone."

"Okay," Montgomery said. "I'll answer if I can. If the questions get embarrassing, though, I might let Willie take over."

"You seem to be taking Elsa Travers' death pretty calmly," Bart said. "Mrs. Mattingly told me you were in love with her."

"Mrs. Mattingly is a sweet, romantic old soul," Montgomery replied. "I wasn't in love with Elsa. I admit I was rather fascinated by her weird, exotic personality. I had never known anyone just like her. I took her out a time or two, that was all. I think I took her out mainly to spite Sandrean. Willie and I have strong likes and dislikes. Sandrean happens to be one of our dislikes. He followed Elsa around like a pet dog and he was old enough to be her father, and also he was a bad influence on her. She was a borderline case. Frankly, I don't think she was entirely sane, with all this belief she had in fortunetelling and mumbo jumbo. This damned magician encouraged her in that. No. I am terribly upset about her death, of course, just as I was terribly upset by the death of little Daphne. But I wasn't in love with Elsa Travers. I've got a girl back home, and as soon as I'm sure this television act of mine has a steady sponsor, I'm going to marry her."

"Why should you dislike Sandrean so much? You've gone so far as to suggest, or have Willie suggest, that Sandrean might be implicated in the murder of Daphne and that he might have pushed Elsa off the roof."

"I'm not responsible for what Woodenhead Willie says," Montgomery answered. "I've told you he's garrulous."

"Garrulous!" Woodenhead Willie piped suddenly. "That's a three-dollar word you're always throwing at me. I don't like it. Woodenhead Willie's not garrulous. Woodenhead Willie's a real smart cookie, that's what he is!"

Montgomery said, "Shut up, Willie. The man doesn't like you." He turned to Hardin. "Maybe I just don't like that Salvador Dali mustache the little man wears," he said.

"That's a pretty frivolous reason for accusing a man of murder."

"I didn't accuse him. I just feel that this Sandrean is one of those weird personalities who is capable of anything and that includes murder. I thought those feathers they found were damned funny in view of the fact that Sandrean has this fixation on a feathered serpent. I liked old Lennox and I don't think he was capable of killing Daphne or anybody else. I was disgusted by the fact that the police were willing to believe he was the murderer without even investigating Sandrean thoroughly. They barely questioned him. I thought that might be a bullet hole in the wall, and I thought somebody's attention ought to be directed to it. I guess Willie thought the same. That's why he gave you those sly hints. He knew you were friendly with this cop, Romano."

Bart said, "I see. I understand you're meeting Adrian Temple tonight. What time are you picking him up?"

"They said he'd be out about five-thirty."

"Will you do something for me?" Bart asked. "Something that might really help Jim Lennox?"

"I suppose so. What is it?"

"Bring Temple to my flat instead of bringing him home from the hospital."

Montgomery hesitated. "I don't know," he said. "Where's your flat?"

"Above Bromberg's Flea Circus and Fun Arcade on Forty-second Street. Do you know the place?"

"Know it?" said Montgomery. "Sure, I know it. Willie and I played a week in the Fun Arcade once when we were short of eating money."

"Will you bring Temple there this evening?"

"I don't know if he would want to come," Montgomery said.

"He'll come if you give him a message from me."

"What message?"

"Tell him I expect his wife's murderer to be in my flat around six o'clock tonight," Bart answered.

nineteen

Dr. Raines, the physician Marty Land had engaged when James Lennox was first taken into custody, knew Dr. Pellman, the City psychiatrist, personally as well as professionally.

Raines was an extremely tall man in his middle thirties. He had attained distinction in his demanding profession at a remarkably early age. He was prematurely bald, a fact he did not regret much, since he thought the baldness made him look older and medicine was one profession in which youthful appearance was actually a handicap. Raines' sunburned face was mobile and handsome and it was warmly lit by his dark, intelligent eyes. He stood now outside Pellman's office. Presently a patient came out and walked by him toward the big ward. Raines did not know that the thin, pale man in the hospital robe was Adrian Temple. He did not go into the office for a few minutes. He waited until a nurse came up and said, "I think it's all right for you to go in now, Doctor. The interview seems to be over."

Raines tapped at the door, opened it and said, "May I come in, George?"

The gaunt psychiatrist was sitting at his desk and he seemed to be in a brown study. He looked up, said, "Why, hello, Irving. Come in, come in."

The office was as stiflingly hot as Lennox's little room. Raines thought of his own comfortable, air-conditioned offices on Central Park. George must be a dedicated man to take this, he told himself. His own practice was fairly opulent now, but he understood something of hardship. He had been a young navy medic in the war.

Raines said, "Even if the city can't afford it, I'd think you'd pay to have an air-conditioner put in. This place is a Turkish bath."

"I confess I've thought of doing so," Pellman replied. "It's a temptation in weather like this. But it would be bad psychology. I have to interview the poor devils in this little coop and sometimes I have to pass pretty drastic judgments on them. I may find them insane and send them away to an

asylum for the rest of their natural lives. Or I may find they're
legally sane and condemn them to the electric chair. They're
full of enough aggressions already. It would never do to have
them think their doctor enjoys special privileges and com-
forts."

Raines seated himself. He said, "I suppose you're right.
George, I don't like the looks of that patient of mine in the
little room down the hall."

"You're attending the old man who's accused of murdering
the girl, aren't you? That man who just went out of here
is her husband. I'm worried about that poor fellow, too."

Raines said, "I'm Marty Land's personal physician. He
asked me to take the old man's case. George, I'm afraid he's
going to die if we keep him here much longer."

The gaunt doctor bit his lip and nodded seriously. "I
know," he said. "One of the residents, Dr. Bell, is alarmed,
too. Of course, he's not my baby, really. I looked in on him
in the ordinary course of things, but the police haven't charged
him and so they haven't asked for a certificate of sanity.
And he was put here because of physical ailments. Bell says
it's more shock than anything else, although he does have a
heart condition. Shock is bad when they're that age."

"I'd like to tell you about him, George," Raines said.
"He has a blood pressure and heart condition, of course,
but otherwise he's a pretty healthy old fellow. With regular
check-ups and fundamental care he can live a fairly active
and healthy life for years. As you know, when they get into
their seventies it's the will to keep going that's the deciding
factor. The spark, that's what counts. If they keep their
interests, they can keep on going a long, long time, even
with complicated ailments, because we've learned a lot
about geriatrics in recent years. This old man has led a blameless life up to now. I'm not competent to judge his guilt
or innocence in this case, but anything this nasty is 'way out
of character. He achieved considerable distinction in the
theatre. He was well adjusted enough to bear up under
poverty. He hasn't any family, but he's had the spark recently
in the form of a little job that gives him minimum security
and a sense of being needed. He's a kind of secretary for a
Broadway newspaperman named Hardin. This accusation has
almost killed him. The spark's burnt down so low it's hardly
glowing at all. And that little room he's in is hot as a boiler.
Can't we get him out of there at least, George?"

Pellman shook his head with frustration. "What can I do?"

he asked. "A murder suspect is supposed to be in a private room. A man with a heart condition who's brought in by police is supposed to be in a private room. He's both. And that's the only private room available in the locked section, even if the others were any better, which they aren't. The truth is, Irving, we've got dozens of patients in the private pavilions paying fifteen and twenty dollars a day and up for rooms that are just about as hot as his. I'll grant you hospitals should be air-conditioned. It would take about ten million dollars to air-condition these rambling buildings. Where are we going to get the money? Who's going to give it to us? You tell me what I can do, Irving. I'd really like to know."

Raines said, "I'm sorry. I didn't mean to criticize. I just thought it might be possible to make him a little bit more comfortable, but maybe that wouldn't really help. We've got to fan that spark back into life somehow. I can't tell you what to do, but I can tell you this. If he has to stay here over one more night, I don't think he'll be alive tomorrow morning. That's the brutal truth."

"Can you suggest any way that I might 'fan the spark,' as you call it?" Pelman asked. "I'm willing to try. God knows, I'm willing to try anything."

"I'm afraid you're as helpless as I am," said Raines. "If I could go in there right now and tell him the police know he is innocent, that they've caught the murderer and he's free to leave, I'm willing to bet that he'd be out of shock in five minutes, that the spark would start glowing bright again. I expect his blood pressure would drop down pretty close to normal, even, inside an hour."

"But we can't do that," said Pellman.

Raines sighed and rose from the chair. He said, "No. We can't do it. I guess it's up to the police or to Marty Land or to this fellow Hardin to save the old man's life. If they're going to do it, they'd better do it pretty quick."

twenty

Hardin left Montgomery and Woodenhead Willie and went downstairs. There was a pay phone in the back hall of the rooming house. He deposited a coin and dialed the number of Manhattan West. He asked for Romano, but Grierson came on the phone.

Grierson said, "The lieutenant went home. It was supposed to be his day off, anyway, but he stuck around until the medics sent him home. The heat has got him beat and his stomach was all upset."

Bart couldn't believe it. "Romano never goes home when a murder case is breaking!" he declared. "He doesn't even go home to sleep. He sleeps on that leather couch in his office."

"Listen, mister," Grierson said, and it was a big speech for the taciturn young detective, "you're like everybody else. You think cops aren't human. They are. They get sick and they feel the heat and sometimes they drop dead on duty. Besides, I guess Romano doesn't figure a murder case *is* breaking. I guess he figures it's broken and they've caught the murderer."

Bart said, "Can you give me his address?"

Grierson hesitated. Finally he said, "I wish you wouldn't bother him. He looked bad when he left. But his address isn't any secret. It's in the Bronx phone book."

He gave Hardin an address in the huge Parkchester housing development in the East Bronx.

Hardin was born on Broadway and he had been to the Bronx exactly three times in his life. Twice his father had taken him to the zoo when he was a child, and once he had seen a ball game at the Yankee Stadium. He almost never used the subway except on the rare occasions when he was deeply in debt and underwent a stringent economy wave. He would have had little idea what train to take to reach the East Bronx, although he had lived in New York all his life. As usual, he depended upon the geographical omniscience of a taxi driver. He caught a cab at Sixth Avenue.

130

The driver said, "Mister, I'll tell you the truth. If I'd known you wanted to go to the Bronx, I'd have passed you up. It's a big take on the meter, but I'll probably come back empty all the way and get lost six times and pick up a ticket on a one-way street. I know we take East River Drive and then try and get to Bruckner Boulevard, but after that I have to look at maps."

"I can't help you with directions," Bart said, "but I can keep you from riding home empty. You can keep the flag up and wait for me."

"It's a funny thing," the driver said, becoming philosophical. "I was born on Tenth Avenue and I'm over forty and I've never been off Manhattan Island in my life, except to attend a war or when I get a fare to the Giants' game or when I visit my in-laws on Staten Island. You know what I read the other day? I read that the Bronx is the only part of New York City that's on the mainland of the United States. All the rest of the damned town is just islands. Ain't that something? I was born in New York and I been here all my life and I've hardly ever been in the United States. Well, you and I will make a trip to the good old U.S.A., mister, just see what it is like."

After a long ride, the cab crossed a bridge over a narrow river. The driver said ceremoniously, "We are now entering the United States of America! I wonder if we got to pass the customs?"

On Bruckner Boulevard, the cabbie pulled to the side of the road twice to consult maps. He finally turned off and headed west, and got lost completely under an elevated-train structure and had to backtrack. At last he found a road that led into the apartment development.

The Parkchester houses were built around a circle and a little park. They seemed vaguely Tudor in design, with dormer windows. They spread for acres and acres and acres. It was a city in itself. The town's big stores had branches in the main square and there was a picture show and all the other necessities of modern urban life within the development itself.

The driver was overawed and no longer seemed to regret the long trip. He was inclined to regard it as an educational tour. "Can you imagine it?" he said. "Can you imagine finding a thing like this 'way up here in the Bronx, U.S.A.? Why, it's just like Peter Cooper and Stuyvesant and all them other developments on Manhattan!"

When they finally found the right house in the maze of facsimile dwellings, Hardin himself got lost in the corridors. When he found the right corridor, he had difficulty finding the right bell. There was a battery of apartment bells that reached from his waist to his head. At last he discovered one marked "Romano."

He took a self-service elevator to the fifth floor.

Romano's wife, who answered the door, was a pleasant-faced, dark-haired, middle-aged woman. Bart introduced himself. She held out her hand to Bart cordially. "Mr. Hardin!" she said. "I've been wanting to meet you so much. I've begged my husband to ask you up, but he says you don't like to leave Broadway unless it's absolutely necessary. Your father used to come up to our old place near here for spaghetti dinners many's the time. He said I cooked the best meat balls in New York."

She led Bart into a large and tastefully furnished apartment. Romano was sprawled out in a chair in the living room, wearing striped pajamas and sipping bicarbonate of soda. His wife had swathed his head in a moist towel.

"Endes!" Mrs. Romano called. "Here's Mr. Hardin to see you."

Endes, Bart thought. So that's Romano's first name. He had never heard it before. That was New York. You knew a man all your life and you didn't know his first name. Bart looked at Romano, said, "You look kind of like Whistler's mother in that mobcap."

Romano said, "Hello, honey boy. I didn't think I was such an invalid I'd be having callers. I hope you didn't bring flowers. That would make me think I'm real sick. My wife says it's just work and the heat that's got me."

Bart sat down. He said, "I had to see you about something. I called the office and they said you were sick, but I had to come up anyway. Are you seriously ill?"

Romano said, "Like I say, it's just the heat and work and a nervous stomach, and besides, it was supposed to be my day off anyway."

Mrs. Romano returned to the room accompanied by a young and dark and very lovely girl.

She said, "Excuse, but you must meet our daughter, Ellie, Mr. Hardin. She is on vacation from Marymount College. Your father was so fond of her. He used to dandle her on his knee when she was a baby and bring her little presents."

Bart rose and smiled at the girl. "Hello, honey," he said. "You're prettier than any showgirl on Broadway."

Ellie blushed.

"I will put the little *espresso* machine on and make strong coffee," Mrs. Romano said. "Strong, hot coffee is best for you in warm weather. All Italians know this. I have just made *crispelli*. Do you know *crispelli*, Mr. Hardin? It is small, fried honey cakes. Your father was so fond of them. They are for saints' days, but the Romanos are all gluttons. They eat *crispelli* the whole year around."

Romano looked at his wife fondly. "Rosa," he said, "the last time they got Hardin off Broadway they had to send him to Korea. He didn't come up here to drink coffee and eat cakes. He came up because he has business."

"Quiet, please, you," his wife replied. "If you are sick, be sick. To be sick is to be quiet. Do not try to bully me. You are not a big, brave policeman now. You are just a foolish man in his pajamas. Business is not as important as nourishment. I will bring *espresso* and *crispelli*."

She led her daughter from the room.

Hardin said to Romano, "I'm sorry to hit you with this when you aren't feeling well. But it's got to be done tonight and there was too much to tell you on the phone. Do you think you can get back into town this evening?"

Romano said, "Why should I?"

"To arrest a murderer. I know who killed Daphne Temple."

Romano sighed. "I might get well real quick if I could arrest a murderer," he answered. "Arresting murderers has got to be kind of a hobby with me. But I'm afraid you're going off the deep end again."

Bart said, "Will you be at my apartment as seven o'clock tonight? That's all I ask."

Romano's reply was interrupted by the entrance of Rosa, who bore coffee and little cakes. For the next quarter of an hour they drank coffee and munched the *crispelli*, which Bart, who had no taste for sweets, found surprisingly delicious. Rosa talked of simple, homely things and urged Bart to force her husband to retire from the force. "He has spent his whole life running after nasty murderers," she said. "He is too old and fat for that now. All it has brought him is a bad stomach. He is still young enough to work in some decent profession that does not keep him away from his home for days on end and give him indigestion."

Rosa finally left them to themselves. She said, "Now you can have your foolish business. Business is best on a full stomach, always."

Romano turned his sad, dark eyes on Bart. "My wife don't think much of cops," he said. "She thinks they're kind of useless. She thinks there wouldn't be any criminals if everybody had a nice home with *espresso* and *crispelli*. That's her answer to everything, *espresso* and *crispelli*. The way she'd run the United Nations is serve them *espresso* and *crispelli* and say, 'Let's all be friends.' She's kind of like you. She's great on short cuts. But short cuts just don't work."

Hardin said, "There has to be a short cut in this."

Romano sighed heavily. "Tell me what you've got," he said.

Bart said, "Today I found a pillow hidden inside a corduroy pillow cover. It was a wonderful place to hide a pillow, because that's right where one belongs, in a pillow cover. It's so obvious that no one would think to look for it there. This pillow was filled with feathers. They were white feathers. I'm pretty sure they were goose feathers. There was a hole burned in the pillow. That was the missing piece. That was all I really needed."

Romano said, "Go on."

Bart talked urgently for a long while. Romano listened and did not interrupt. He merely grunted occasionally.

When Bart had finished, Romano shook his head. He said, "It's a real good theory. I think it's the right one. It's along the lines that I've been thinking myself. And the pillow is important. But you still don't understand. You can't get impatient in a murder case. You have to let things take their course. You have to wait for the breaks, no matter how nervous your duodenal gets. There's only one way to catch a murderer. You do it by the book."

Bart said, "We haven't got time to do it by the book."

"So you want me to come to your apartment at seven?" Romano asked. "You're going to have it all wrapped up by then, is that it?"

"That's it," Bart answered. "A certain person is coming to my flat at six. And I've asked Montgomery to bring Adrian Temple there."

Romano said, "All right. I guess I'm going to lead for you with my poor sore chin again. I hope I won't be sorry."

"That's all I want," Hardin answered.

Bart found Mrs. Romano and her daughter in the kitchen

and bade them good-by. Mrs. Romano pressed a paper sack filled with *crispelli* upon him.

Hardin and the cab driver ate *crispelli* all the way to Manhattan. It was only twenty to four when they turned off Bruckner Boulevard and crossed the little bridge again. The cab driver had taken an hour to reach Parkchester, but now he knew the way he made much better time. Bart could do nothing before six. He decided he might as well drop by the office for an hour or so and help Pops Taylor out. He directed the driver to the *Broadway Times*. When they arrived there, the fare on the meter was nearly ten dollars. Hardin felt so good he gave the driver twenty.

Pops Taylor told him that the good thing in the third at Aqueduct had lost. Moe Selig must be burning, Hardin thought. He could have won thousands for the book if he had followed his gambler's hunch instead of his businessman's discretion.

Hardin remained at the office until five-thirty, reading copy, writing heads and making up early-closing forms in the composing room, but his mind was hardly on his work. Pete Cruise came down with the print of Chloe's picture. Bart sized it and sent it to engraving.

At five-thirty, he turned the paper over to Pops Taylor again. He told Pops to make the cut of Chloe a "must." He left the office and walked down Eighth Avenue to his flat above the flea circus. The sense of excitement that amounted almost to euphoria which he had felt upon leaving Romano had deserted him now. He was gnawed by doubt. So many things could still go wrong. And an old man's life was in his hands.

Back in his apartment, Bart poured himself a stiff drink, the first of the day. He took half a dozen sheets of typewriter paper from a drawer and placed them on the desk. He made sure a fountain pen was filled and placed it beside the paper.

He found the little Waldman twenty-five he had taken from Elsa Travers. He checked it and dropped it in his pocket.

Then he sat down and waited, and it seemed an endless vigil. Despite the floor fan, the big old room was viciously hot. Perspiration poured from him.

At six o'clock exactly there was a knock on the door.

Moe Selig had been wrong. Stony Martin could still tell time when he was looking at a clock.

twenty-one

When Hardin opened the door, Stony Martin stood stock-still for a moment and stared at him. There was no expression on his ugly-baby face unless it was one of wariness. He said, "Selig said you wanted me."

Hardin said, "Come in, Martin."

When Martin was in the room Hardin asked, "Are you packing a gun, Stony?"

Martin shook his head. "Selig said I shouldn't bring one. Selig said it was a muscle job."

"You don't mind if I make sure, do you?" Bart asked. He patted Stony's pockets. Stony obviously didn't like it, but he submitted to it. He said, "I don't like people putting their hands on me, mister. But Selig said it was a job and I was to do whatever you told me. So I'm doing it. I work for Benny Speakman. He used to be my manager when I was a fighter. Benny works for Selig. So I'll do what Selig says. But I ain't forgetting, mister. I ain't forgetting what you did to me and to the girl. Keep that in mind. The day is gonna come. I ain't forgetting."

Hardin said, "What do you think I did to the girl, Stony?"

"She went off a roof. Maybe she was pushed."

"All right, Stony," Hardin said after he had finished examining his pockets. "You're clean. You haven't got a gun. But I've got one." He showed Stony the little Waldman twenty-five. "Maybe you remember it, Stony. Elsa Travers said you gave it to her. I'm keeping it handy just in case you blow your top and forget what Selig told you."

Stony said, "I won't forget what Selig told me. Not today. This ain't the day, but the day is coming, mister. I got to get back in the fight game. Selig can get me a fight any time he wants to. I got to get back to fighting. I still got what it takes."

Stony threw a hard right cross into the air.

"How old are you, Martin?" Hardin asked.

"Thirty-seven. It ain't too old. Look at old Joe Walcott.

136

He won the champeenship when he was over forty. He said he was younger, but he was over forty. And look at old Archie Moore. I ain't too old. I'm good as I ever was. I could have been the champ, but they wouldn't turn me loose. They kept on promising they'd turn me loose, but they never did. But I can make a comeback."

Hardin poured whisky from the Irish bottle. "Do you want a drink?" he asked.

"Not me. I never touched a drop of liquor or smoked a cigarette. Drinking and smoking ain't good for fighters. I still go to Stillman's Gym three times a week and punch the bag and skip the rope. All I need is a little roadwork to leg me up. I'm as good as I ever was. That's why I took this job. That's why I ain't going to belt you, mister, in spite of what you done last night. I can't get Selig mad. You got to have Selig back of you in this town if you're a fighter. Selig's name don't get in the sporting news, but he runs the fight game in this town. I can wait for you, mister. I can wait as long as I've got to wait."

"That reassuring," Bart said. "I'm good at waiting, too, Stony. And I don't forget too easily. I can remember a few things you did recently. Things with guns."

"You can't prove nothing," Stony declared. "That little gun you got is one I just give the girl to protect herself with. It wasn't the gun that killed that dancer. It wasn't the gun was used by whoever tried to chill you last night."

Bart said, "I guess we understand each other. It's what they call an armed truce—for today. I kicked your face in last night and you didn't like it much and you think I shoved your girl off a roof. You tried to kill me with a gun. We'll both forget—today. Okay? Sit down and relax."

Stony looked puzzled. He sat down, but his eyes remained on Hardin. "Selig said to do what you told me," he said. "I'm sitting down."

Bart looked searchingly at the ex-fighter's blank and battered face. There was a bruise on the cheekbone and a split lip and a missing front tooth as a result of the booting Hardin had given him the night before. Hardin didn't feel too proud of himself. Despite Stony's size and his obvious animal strength he did not, somehow, seem formidable. He just seemed pitifully helpless and confused.

Bart took the little Waldman from his pocket again.

"This wasn't the only gun you gave the girl, Stony," he

said. "You didn't give her this one until last night. The other
gun you gave her was an army forty-five. It was an army forty-
five that killed Daphne Temple."

Puffy scar tissue had permanently welted the flesh around
Stony's eyes and narrowed them. Stony squeezed them more
closely shut as he glared at Hardin.

"Listen, mister. Selig said this was a job. A muscle job.
He said he'd pay me fifty bucks for it if you was satisfied.
He didn't say I had to answer questions."

So Selig is keeping a hundred and a half of the fee for
his Old Bookmakers' Home, Bart thought, grinning wryly.

"I didn't ask you a question, Stony," Bart said. "I just
made a statement."

Stony said, as if he were trying to convince himself, "You
ain't got nothing on me."

"I know one thing about you for sure, Stony. I know you'd
do anything that girl Elsa told you to do. That included
shooting people."

Stony's scrambled brains did not function very rapidly.
He had to think about it for a while. Finally he said, "I
think you're trying to frame me, Hardin. It was just a gag,
you telling Selig you had a muscle job for me."

"I've got a job for you," Bart assured him.

"What kind of job?"

"I'm not worrying about your attack on me. You missed
and I gave you the boot and I've forgotten the whole thing
already. But I'm going to get a confession from the murderer of Daphne Temple, Stony. I don't care how I get it.
But I'm going to get it pretty quick now, no matter what I
have to do."

Stony's scrambled brains were still pondering that one
when there was a knock on the door.

Stony jumped up from the chair instinctively and backed
up to a table that stood against the wall.

Bart said, "Don't be frightened, Stony. This is Daphne
Temple's husband. He's going to be in on the confession."

Hardin opened the door. Montgomery and Temple were
waiting outside. Temple seemed white and sick. A muscle
in his face was twitching. Bart stood aside and admitted
Temple into the room. Then he blocked the door with his
body and kept Montgomery from entering. He said, "Thanks,
Montgomery. I'm afraid I can't ask you in. This is kind of
private."

Montgomery obviously was curious and wanted to come in, too. "This is a hell of a way to treat me after I've gone to all the trouble of bringing him," he complained. "Why can't I meet Daphne's murderer, too?"

"No," said Bart. "I'm sorry."

"But Mrs. Mattingly will be sore at me. I promised I'd take good care of Adrian and bring him right home from the hospital."

Bart said, "I'll take care of him. Good-by, Montgomery. Give my regards to Woodenhead Willie."

He closed the door in Montgomery's face.

Temple was standing just inside the door, staring across the big room at Martin's hulking figure.

He said to Bart, "Is this the man? Is this the man who killed my wife?"

Bart said, "This is Stony Martin. He used to be a fighter. He works as bouncer at a club where Elsa Travers danced, the Seventh Veil. He was in love with Elsa. He would do anything she asked him to do. That included shooting people. Stony deals in hot guns. He gave Elsa the gun that killed Daphne. He could have borrowed it back the night Daphne was killed, of course."

Stony said, "Damn you, mister. I knew this was a frame."

Temple seemed dazed. He said at last. "That poor old man. That poor old man went through all that torture and he didn't kill her. I couldn't believe he had."

"Yes," said Hardin. "Elsa and her boy friend didn't give a damn about the old man's suffering. They didn't give a damn about the possibility of him dying, even. They were too concerned with their own skins. That's one reason I can't feel too bad about hounding Elsa into suicide. She could take it only up to a certain point. But she was even nasty to the end. She didn't leave a note that would have saved old Lennox. And she put a little pin, a little Feathered Serpent, that she'd never worn before, on her dress. That could have made Sandrean, who gave it to her, seem suspicious. It could have been a sort of tip that Sandrean was with her when she went off the roof, because everyone in the house knew about the pin and knew she never wore it and might have thought she had some reason for wearing it the night she died. But I don't believe she really tried to implicate Sandrean. I think it was just this crazy superstition of hers. They'd found feathers around Daphne's body, and Sandrean said the Feathered Serpent was a symbol of evil and revenge, and so she pinned the Feathered Serpent on her breast before she killed herself."

"Elsa," said Adrian Temple softly. "I can't believe it."

The three men were still standing. Hardin said, "Let's sit down. I'll tell you how your wife was killed, Temple. It's going to take a little while."

Temple collapsed into a chair. Bart seated himself between Martin and the door. Martin stood tense and silent for a moment. Finally he sat down, too.

Bart reached for whisky. He poured some into his glass. He said to Temple, "Do you want a drink, Adrian, or has the stuff caused you enough grief already?"

Temple said, "I don't want a drink."

Bart sipped his whisky. The hand that was not holding the glass touched the little pistol in his pocket. It was comforting to feel its weight and solidity.

"Elsa Travers was in love with you, Adrian," Hardin said. "You know that, of course. Your wife stood in the way. There was additional motive. She knew about the twenty-five-thousand-dollar insurance policy and that things were going bad with the act. Killing Daphne might mean that she could get you and that you'd have twenty-five thousand when you started out together. She'd had a couple of dates with Martin when she worked at the club. She knew he sold hot guns. She knew she could wrap him around her little finger, that he would do anything she asked him. So she got a gun from him, an army forty-five. She didn't know that Stony had to report the name of every person who got one of his guns, because the Syndicate wanted to make sure they didn't go into the wrong hands. Stony is afraid of Selig and the Syndicate. He didn't dare not to report the one he gave to Elsa, but he reported it as a regular sale. Selig told me about it.

"Elsa wanted Daphne dead, but she couldn't do the thing herself. She had to have an accomplice who would actually commit the murder. She set it up so she'd have a perfect alibi. The trouble was, the accomplice wanted an alibi, too. The murder wasn't committed at the time Mrs. Mattingly heard the shot. Daphne had been dead a little while when Mrs. Mattingly and Elsa returned from the Music Hall. Not long enough for the medical evidence to show that she wasn't killed at the time the shot was heard. The medical evidence was particularly difficult to establish with any exactitude, anyway, because of Daphne's paralysis. Daphne was killed about half an hour before the body was discovered. The murderer left the weapon concealed in the room in some prearranged, easily available place. When Mrs. Mattingly and Elsa got home, Elsa went directly upstairs. She opened the door of Daphne's room, got the gun and fired a shot through the open window into the wall of the house next door. She threw the gun out the window and it landed on the fire escape. Of course she had on gloves, so her prints wouldn't be on the gun. The whole thing took only a few seconds. She closed the door, stood in the hall and screamed as if she'd just heard the shot, along with Mrs. Mattingly. When Mrs. Mattingly rushed upstairs, they found Jim Lennox out on the fire escape. That was an unexpected bonus for Elsa and her accomplice. He wasn't supposed to be home at all, but it worked out that he was a ready-made suspect for them. The time of the shot that presumably killed Daphne was set like that so that the man who actually fired it could establish an iron-bound alibi for himself for a few minutes to eleven on the night of the murder.

"I set it up so a fortuneteller would work on Elsa and tell her that I knew she had procured a gun from Stony Martin. I wanted to see what she would do. What she did was go to Stony and arrange to have me killed. Also, she was afraid that the fortuneteller and others might know about her getting the gun from Stony originally. So she provided herself with an alibi for that. She had Stony give her another gun, a Waldman twenty-five that couldn't have fired the shot that killed Elsa. That would explain the gun she got from Stony, in case there were questions from other sources."

Temple said, "For God's sake, Hardin! Why don't you turn this man over to the police? Why do you just let him sit there? He's dangerous. He can escape. He—he can *hurt* us!"

"I'm not turning Martin over to the cops," Bart answered calmly. "I asked him here for another reason. He was Elsa's stooge and he gave her the gun that killed Daphne and he tried to murder me, but that doesn't bother me too much. Stony Martin didn't kill your wife.

"You killed Daphne, Adrian."

twenty-two

Stony Martin had been sitting quietly at the far end of the room in the shadows, his eyes darting suspiciously from Hardin to Temple. Now he spoke suddenly and unexpectedly, blurting out the words.

"You got it all wrong, mister. She wasn't carrying any torch for this jerk. He was just her dancing partner. She wanted a man. She and I was going to get married as soon as I got straightened out with Selig and began to fight again. She wasn't in on this kill, with him or nobody. She didn't get that gun to chill the dame, She got it from me a couple of months ago, maybe more. She said some little greaseball in the house was annoying her, making passes, and she was scared of him. I wanted to work him over, but she wouldn't let me. She just wanted a gun to scare him off was all. The only heaters I had then were these forty-fives that the boys on the docks had just broke out of an army shipment to Germany. She told me the old man must have stole the gun from her room to chill this Temple dame. She told me you'd found out the heater belonged to her and there was going to be trouble and she was going to get arrested for murder. That's why I tried to fix it so you'd stay nice and quiet. You was right about the other gun, the little pea-shooter you got in your pocket now. She said if somebody else knew about her having got a gun from me she had to be able to show 'em some gun that didn't kill the dame. So I give her that. It's too small to be much use to the guys who buy from me, anyway. The guys who buy from me want to make a nice, big hole when they squeeze a trigger."

Bart said, "She was in love with Temple, Stony. She was just playing you for a sucker, using you. Now, Temple, I'm going to tell you exactly what I know, exactly how it happened, and then I'm going to ask you to do something. If you don't do what I ask, it won't be pleasant."

Temple said frantically, "This is all wrong! I wasn't anywhere near the house the night it happened. I was wandering around drunk. I thought I'd killed my wife the night before. I must have been with you when she was shot, Hardin."

"You planned it a long time, Temple," Hardin asserted. "Ever since you began your affair with Elsa. It's possible you planned it two years ago and that the car smash was an attempt to murder her. About six months ago you got a real bright idea. You'd heard about these harmless crackpots who wander into police stations and confess to every crime that's ever been committed, including the kidnapping of the long-lost Charlie Ross. You knew the police didn't take 'em seriously. You knew they never got anything except a few days in the psycho ward. So you hit on what you thought was a perfect setup. You'd confess a murder at a time that would provide you with a perfect alibi for that same murder. You led up to the big event last winter by going to Homicide and confessing to Romano that you'd murdered your wife at a time you knew they'd find she was quite alive. That would mark you as a crackpot. All they did was send you to City for a few days. They just marked you down as an alcoholic who had delusions. That prepared the stage.

"You had Elsa get this gun from Stony and keep it hidden until it was time to use it. You waited until conditions were perfect for you. You could afford to wait. If things went just right, you were going to get away with murder. You were going to rid yourself of an invalid wife who was an encumbrance to you. You were going to get Elsa and twenty-five thousand untaxable insurance dollars. It would cost you only a little inconvenience, a few more days in the City psycho ward. Your idea was to have an unprejudiced witness like Mrs. Mattingly hear the shot and discover the body at a time when you couldn't possibly have committed the murder because you were making a confession to the police or to someone the police trusted at that exact moment. It took a little doing, but your patience was rewarded. Sandrean offered you the perfect setup. When he got on the bill at the Music Hall, he gave tickets for the performance to every person in the house, except Daphne, of course, who couldn't attend because she was confined to her wheelchair. You pretended you were going to the theatre with the others.

"In the meantime, you had started going out and drinking and staying away for a day or so, so that it wouldn't seem odd for you to disappear when the crucial time arrived. The night before the theatre party, you probably took enough liquor to give yourself a breath and you put on your drunk act and made sure that Mrs. Mattingly saw you stagger out of the house. She called it 'one of your little disappearances' and thought little of it.

"I don't know where you stayed that night or the next day. It doesn't matter much. You may have staggered in and out of a few bars where you were known and had a drink at each of them to bolster your story of wandering around in a drunken daze in case the police checked. You may have rented a room in some cheap hotel where they didn't know you and didn't ask questions, and holed up for the whole time.

"The big tip-off was that you and Elsa attended the show at the Music Hall a few days before the murder. You had no reason to do that, since you were planning to see it in a couple of nights with the others. You went there so you could time it exactly, to make sure that you would be in the right place at the right time, when the second shot was fired. You went to the Gypsy tearoom to talk over your final plans and Alma Turner overheard you discussing the show at the Music Hall and Sandrean's Feathered Serpent act.

"It wouldn't be too difficult for Elsa to pretend that it was all right to leave Daphne alone. She'd been left alone in the house before and she'd been all right. She could move around in her wheelchair and get anything she needed. And Elsa and the others would be home in time to help her into bed. You also had to rely upon Elsa to keep the others downstairs while she went up and fired the gun out the window and screamed. That wouldn't be hard, either. Elsa was an ingenious girl. All she had to do was suggest they have a pitcher of iced tea in the parlor, or, perhaps, buy some ice cream on the way home. Then she could run upstairs on the pretense of looking in on Daphne and there would have been Mrs. Mattingly, Lennox and Montgomery besides herself to witness the time the shot was fired and the body was discovered.

"Then the plan went wrong, and it must have driven Elsa frantic, because I doubt that she had any way of getting in touch with you. Old Jim Lennox got sick from the heat and couldn't attend the theatre with the others. It wasn't as bad as it might have been, however. You were pretty certain to make sure there was no one in the house before you killed your wife. If there'd been anyone there, you could have

simply played the role of a drunk coming home at last.
Checking the rooms was easy because of the heat wave. Most
of the doors were left ajar for ventilation.

"You must have gone into the house a little after ten.
It had to be then, because Sandrean came home to get a
spare set of teeth and he didn't leave until ten. Maybe you
were watching the house and saw him go in and come out.
You found Lennox snoring on his bed. He had taken some
tablets that were mildly sedative. Daphne was sleeping in her
wheelchair. Elsa had doubtless given her medicine before
she left and she probably gave her an extra amount of
sedation. Anyway, Sandrean saw her sleeping just a few
minutes before you came into the house.

"Despite Lennox being there, you decided to go through
with it. There was a key on the outside of Lennox's door.
You closed the door and turned the key. But you had an
unexpected problem. You didn't want the shot to awaken
Lennox. You didn't have a silencer. For a direct contact
shot, a feather pillow is a pretty fair muffler. The shot would
be audible, of course, but it probably wouldn't be loud enough
to awaken Lennox and it would hardly be discernible from
street noises. You didn't want to use a pillow from either of
the beds in the room, because a missing pillow or one with a
hole in it would attract notice and would direct attention to
a muffled shot, which might have been fatal to you. So you got
a pillow from the linen closet in the hall. Mrs. Mattingly
trusted her roomers and thought of them as members of the
family and didn't lock things up. The pillow you got was a
new one stuffed with goose feathers. You had the problem
of getting rid of the pillow after you'd fired the gun through
it. You took a kapok pillow on the day bed out of a zipper
cover and put it in the linen closet.

"You muffled the gun in the pillow, placed it against your
wife's heart and fired. Feathers spewed out, of course, and you
didn't have time to clean them all up. Some stuck to the
wound and fell on your wife's clothes and the floor and a few
drifted out the window onto the fire escape. You hid the
feather pillow in the corduroy cover from which you had
removed the kapok pillow.

"I suspect you killed your wife about ten-twenty. You
figured you could be at the Sligo Slasher's bar with your
phony confession in ten minutes. I guess I'm an old fogey
whose habits are pretty well known. You thought it was

almost certain you'd find me drinking Irish there at that hour. But even if you didn't, you were safe. You'd probably found out some way from Jim Lennox that Romano was on duty and you had time to get to Manhattan West before the second shot was fired, so he could be your alibi. Or you might have done it with plenty of time to spare by going to a nearer precinct station and telling your story to the desk sergeant or a detective. You'd given yourself about half an hour to spare. The medical examiner wouldn't arrive for a while after the body was found, and the half-hour hiatus between the shots would have made the medical evidence as to time of death seem rasonable enough.

"I had been drinking in the Slasher's bar when I heard about the floater from a steerer. Maclaren, who owns the bar, knew where I was and told you. The garage where I was shooting craps was a three-minute walk from the gin mill. You caught me about twenty-five to eleven, maybe a little later, and we were in a bar on Ninth Avenue at the time Elsa was scheduled to fire the shot. You were careful to point out the exact time to me on a big clock on the wall.

"Elsa and Mrs. Mattingly got home as scheduled. Montgomery had left them to have a drink, but Mrs. Mattingly was witness enough. I doubt if Elsa believed you had gone through with the murder, but she found you had and so she played her part. It was simple. She had gloves in her purse. She put them on. She got the gun from a place you had agreed to leave it, fired it through the window. She threw the gun through the window, but it hit the fire escape and stayed there. Jim Lennox remembered the metallic clang it made just after the shot.

"Elsa had nothing else to do but take her gloves off, drop them in her pocketbook, step out into the hall, close the door and start screaming. It was all over in a matter of seconds. Then, when she and Mrs. Mattingly opened the door again, there was Lennox, a ready-made suspect, standing on the fire escape. Elsa was quick to take advantage of this unexpected situation. Lennox said the door of his room was locked. As soon as Mrs. Mattingly rushed downstairs, to call the police, Elsa stepped out into the hall and unlocked the door. When Mrs. Mattingly tried the door, it was unlocked."

Hardin finished the whisky in his glass.

"That's the story, Adrian," he said. "That's the way you killed your wife. There's a stack of paper and a fountain pen on the desk. I want you to sit down at the desk and write it out, just the way it happened. Put in every detail. Then sign the confession."

"I can't!" Adrian exclaimed. "You're trying to save the old man and you'll do anything to get him free. But I didn't kill her! It's all fantastic. I thought I had killed her the night before, but it was just a drunken delusion. The doctors at the hospital said so."

Hardin spoke very calmly. "All right, Adrian. There's an alternative. That's why Stony Martin's here. He's the alternative. He's got orders to do what I tell him to do. If he forgets his orders, I can still control him, because I've got a gun in my pocket. If you write out the confession, I'll see he doesn't touch you. If you don't, I'll walk out of the room and give you to him. He doesn't like you much. You were the lover of a girl he wanted to marry. He was a fighter and he can get pretty cruel. There's one thing about you that isn't phony, Temple. Your fear of pain. Even the doctors admit your fear of pain is real, a phobia. I'm giving you a choice. You can write out the confession or I give you to Stony."

"I can't! I can't do it!" Adrian's voice was shrill.

Bart shrugged. "It's your choice, Adrian," he said. He walked to a phonograph and put a rock n' roll record on the machine. He turned the volume up high.

"Why are you doing that?" Adrian asked, his hysterical voice cutting through the crashing sound of the phonograph record.

"Because I don't want anybody to hear you screaming," Bart answered.

He shouted across the room to Martin, "All right, Stony. I'm leaving. He's all yours. Get up and earn your money. But remember, I don't want him killed."

Stony rose slowly from the chair. Adrian Temple's frightened eyes stared at him. Stony took a pair of black leather gloves from his pocket. He began to slide them on his hands.

"Why is he putting gloves on?" screamed Temple as the music rose to ear-splitting crescendo.

"Because he doesn't like to bruise his knuckles," Bart shouted at Adrian as he turned his back and walked toward the bedroom.

Martin walked slowly toward Temple, moving on the balls of his feet, smacking his gloved right fist into his gloved left palm.

Hardin had reached the bedroom door when Temple

caught him and grabbed him by the shoulders. "For God's sake stop him! For God's sake turn that music off!" he cried. "I'll do what you want!"

Bart shoved Temple away, switched off the recording machine.

Martin was still advancing toward the quaking Temple, his eyes dead and hard.

"I want him," Martin said. "You gave him to me and I'm going to take him."

Temple began to scream. He ran behind Bart.

Martin was moving forward, his body balanced, stalking Temple slowly.

"No, Stony," Bart said. "It's all over. Go sit down. Remember what Selig told you."

"I want him," Martin repeated, and took another step.

Bart took the little Waldman from his pocket. "Don't come any closer, Stony," he warned. "If you do, I'll shoot you. I'll shoot you through the leg. You'll be crippled and you'll never fight again."

Martin shook his head like a fighter who has just taken a hard one on the jaw. His dead eyes went to Bart. He said, "I thought it was a job. Selig said it was a job."

"Selig told you to take my orders. I'm ordering you to go sit down."

Martin walked back across the big room to the chair he had just left. He was pulling off his gloves.

Hardin pushed Temple toward the desk.

Temple sat down, picked up the fountain pen and began to write.

Hardin stood beside him and watched the blue-black words appear on the white paper, the words that would free Jim Lennox if only it was not too late.

He had timed it almost perfectly.

Romano knocked on the door just as Adrian Temple signed the confession.

Grierson was with Romano. They came into the room and Hardin said, "Here's your murderer, Lieutenant. And here's his confession."

Romano wasn't looking at Temple. He was looking at Stony Martin. He said, "Who's this lug? I know his face."

"Just a friend," Bart replied. "He dropped around to chat about the sonnets of Elizabeth Barrett Browning."

Bart turned to Stony. "You'd better go now," he said.

"Tell our friend that I was satisfied. Drop around again some time. We'll have tea and discuss the poetry of Emily Dickinson."

Stony got to his feet and shambled across the big room. He did not look at the two policemen. Grierson stood in his path indecisively, his eyes questioning Romano.

Romano said, "Let him go. You watch Temple for a minute."

Romano took the confession from Bart, but he didn't look at it. He nodded toward the bedroom door, said, "Inside."

Bart followed the detective to the bedroom. Romano pushed the door.

"It was like I was afraid it was going to be," he said. "I know that lug. An old palooka. I saw him fight. He sells hot guns, but we can't make it stick against him. You muscled Temple into the confession. A good lawyer will shoot holes all through it. It doesn't mean a thing. It's like I told you. You've got to do it by the book."

Bart says, "It means something. He says the pillow that muffled the gun is in that corduroy case. He couldn't know that if he hadn't put it there. The pillow is your corroborative evidence. All you've got to do is go and find it officially."

Romano started to protest further, but he was interrupted. Grierson shoved his head through the door. "Temple wants a drink of water," Grierson said. "He's got a headache and he wants to take an aspirin."

Romano shoved Grierson and rushed through the door. "Don't let him take a pill!" he roared.

But he was too late.

Adrian Temple had already taken a pill that wasn't aspirin.

He stood tottering, his hands clutching his belly, his eyes glazed. There was a queer smile on his face. He said faintly, "Dying—hardly hurts at all. . . ."

Then he collapsed to the floor. Grierson dropped down beside him.

For several minutes there was dead silence in the room as Grierson worked on Temple. Grierson looked up at Romano, an expression of disbelief on his face.

"He's dead," he said. "He's dead already."

"He was afraid of pain and he carried his own antidote," Bart said. "He must have had the poison hidden in his clothes, even while he was in the hospital."

Romano looked down sadly at the body on the floor.

He said, "I told you. I told you you never catch a murderer unless you do it by the book."

"We caught this murderer," Bart declared.

Romano shook his head. "Uh-uh," he said. "This murderer escaped."

twenty-three

It had taken some doing on the part of Romano and Marty Land, but it was little more than an hour before all the necessary red tape of releasing James Lennox from custody was completed.

It was eight-thirty when Romano and Bart arrived at City. New York has daylight-saving time in summer and there was still murky daylight at this hour. Marty Land and Dr. Raines were waiting for them at the entrance to the hospital.

Land said, "The doctor thought it would be better if he gave old Jim the news. Sometimes good news is almost as great a shock as bad news."

"How is he?" Bart asked the doctor.

"I've seen it happen many times," the doctor answered, "but every time it's like a miracle, bringing a dead man back to life. In the war it was blood transfusions. They'd bring them down from battle stations and they'd have no blood pressure and no pulse and then they'd get the transfusion and you could see the life flowing back into them. You could see it happen in front of your eyes. Drugs like Coramine and adrenalin have the same effect sometimes. It was just like that with Lennox. I told him the news and I watched him coming back to life. He'll be ready in a few minutes. They couldn't find an orderly and a young off-duty intern named Bell is helping him to dress and check out. I think this Bell is working off a guilt complex. He thought Lennox was guilty and he's doing penance now."

The doctor turned to Bart.

"It might be a good idea to take him to an air-conditioned hotel tonight. And it would be wise to get him to the country for a week or two if it is possible."

"I'll rent a suite in the Waldorf Tower," Bart declared, silently thanking Lady Luck for his bonanza in the floating game. "And I know an old fighter who has a health farm in the country. I'll send him up there for as long as necessary."

Marty Land was looking up at one of the trees with withered foliage. The branches of the tree were thick and lumpy with pigeons that had gone to roost. The roosting pigeons had the hunched and waiting look of bedraggled vultures.

"Maybe we won't need air conditioning tonight," Land said. "Did you know I was a nature student, Doc? Thoreau and Audubon are my favorite authors. Whenever pigeons go to roost like that, it's a sign it's going to rain and the temperature is going to drop. I think the heat wave's over."

A plump pigeon in the tree was molting. It preened itself and one of its feathers drifted down and brushed against Romano's cheek.

Romano jumped and swiped at his cheek with his hand.

Bart grinned at the swarthy detective. He and Romano were friends again.

"What's the matter, copper?" Bart asked. "It's nothing to worry about. It's just a little feather."

www.ingramcontent.com/pod-product-compliance
Lightning Source LLC
Chambersburg PA
CBHW020647180626
46816CB00003B/1168